MW01484068

CHRISTMAS
AT THE
WOMEN'S
HOTEL

ALSO BY DANIEL M. LAVERY

CHRISTMAS
AT THE
WOMEN'S
HOTEL

A Biedermeier Story

DANIEL M. LAVERY

HarperVia

An Imprint of HarperCollins*Publishers*

CHRISTMAS AT THE WOMEN'S HOTEL. Copyright © 2025 by Daniel M. Lavery. All rights reserved. Printed in the United States of America. No part of this book may be used or reproduced in any manner whatsoever without written permission except in the case of brief quotations embodied in critical articles and reviews. For information, address HarperCollins Publishers, 195 Broadway, New York, NY 10007. In Europe, HarperCollins Publishers, Macken House, 39/40 Mayor Street Upper, Dublin 1, D01 C9W8, Ireland.

HarperCollins books may be purchased for educational, business, or sales promotional use. For information, please email the Special Markets Department at SPsales@harpercollins.com.

harpercollins.com

FIRST EDITION

Designed by Yvonne Chan
Letters illustration © indigo.arty/Shutterstock
All other illustrations © Natalya Levish/Shutterstock

Library of Congress Cataloging-in-Publication Data has been applied for.

ISBN 978-0-06-345501-6

25 26 27 28 29 LBC 5 4 3 2 1

For Lily and Grace:
And these things write we unto you,
that your joy may be full.

—I JOHN 1:4

AUTHOR'S NOTE

In the real world, Dick Button's Ice-Travaganza exhibit at the New York World's Fair closed in July 1964. In the world of the Biedermeier, it limped along until November 1965. To the best of my knowledge, I have taken no other intentional liberties with the historical record. Any other anachronisms or inconsistencies are the result of careless research habits and a general inattention to detail.

THE SOCIAL REGISTER SET

Chapter One

F or the inhabitants of New York's Biedermeier Hotel for Women, Christmas meant work, and work meant money. During ordinary times, employment came to them fitfully, reluctantly, and often only after tremendous exertion (when it came at all), but between the feasts of All Saints in November and Epiphany in January, nearly any girl who wished for something profitable to occupy her afternoons could make her choice almost at her leisure. The city was lousy with opportunity in winter, and for several months every department store, boutique, and commercial concern in Midtown was absolutely desperate for girls.

They needed girls to dress the windows at Lord & Taylor, Macy's, Gimbels, Bonwit Teller, and Henri Bendel, to say nothing of the sub-carriage trade shops; girls to manage the Christmas markets in the various remaining Scandinavian pocket neighborhoods; girls to assist sales clerks at the greeting card stores on Forty-Second Street; girls to usher, distribute programs, and sell candy and cigarettes at the Radio City Christmas Spectacular and the Broadway shows; and girls to press and fold for the wardrobe head of *The Nutcracker* at the Lincoln Center. Girls who would be considered unemployable at any other time of year (and it was largely this type who inhabited the Biedermeier)—those without experience, training, education, or a pair of gloves not obviously mended—were nevertheless in some indefinite sense commercially essential to the Christmas season.

Yet, even taking this employment boom into account, the Biedermeier's longtime manager, Mrs. Mossler, was startled by this year's prosperity. Mrs. Mossler had awoken in darkness. She usually overtook the morning sun sometime in early September, and it would not match her pace again until late April. After her usual thirteen minutes of Swedish floor exercises, a double-time march up and down the lobby stairs, repeated until just before perspiration threatened, and a highball glass of tomato juice, she was seated at the writing desk in her office, reviewing her accounts with suspicion.

The annual surge of the hotel's residents into the black was not to her an unfamiliar phenomenon, but she had expected only a modest increase. Instead she saw opulence, *brass* opulence, and that at a shocking scale. Carol Lipscomb and Patricia De Boer had both exited arrears in perfect synchronization for the first time in eight months; J.D. Boatwright for the first time in ten. Even Lucianne Caruso—whom she had long known to contribute punctually but rarely comprehensively on the first of each month, who frequently economized on rent whenever work was slack or one of her articles stalled with a new editor—had handed over, in an air of queenly condescension, a check that cleared all outstanding balances.

Mrs. Mossler found herself writing "Paid in full" next to almost every name on the Biedermeier's books in slow, deliberate amazement. And only this morning Kitty Milham, without hint or threat of force, had voluntarily given her three dollars to cover the breaking of a lamp.

But it was not a pleased amazement. Mrs. Mossler had seen too many hotel Christmases to trust this kind of sudden corporate good fortune. Even taking luck into account, it simply was not possible for so many to be doing so well at once without resorting to criminal enterprise.

Mrs. Mossler's ideas about crime were rather hazy, having had very little firsthand experience herself, but she was certain that anything that might be called an enterprise was certain to harbor crime lurking at no great distance.

She was certain that something was amiss with Carol and Patricia. The two lived together in a suite on the eleventh floor. Carol was a student of the classics at Hunter College, while Patricia worked for the Transit Authority, and rare was the day that could produce a nickel between them. In Carol's case this was because she made no money, and in Patricia's because she spent hers as fast as she could make it on art supplies—although Patricia's art was of the upsetting and ultramodern variety, so "supplies" for her might one week have been a dozen broken bathroom mirrors and, the next, material for stringing animal teeth into an old parure case. Lately both girls had grown secretive and close, often staying behind their locked door for days at a time, when ordinarily they held it open for visitors every afternoon. Mrs. Mossler, though concerned, would never use her own keys to set her fears to rest. She respected the privacy of her tenants enormously and would not force her way in anywhere she had not been invited.

Of course, there were other ready sources of cash at this time of year besides holiday employment. There were real

Christmas bonuses—new bills bound together inside neat brown envelopes—or sometimes bottles of good dark liquor for the girls with year-round jobs. Even for the most hopelessly idle among them, there were almost always presents from home. Stephen Wright, who operated the Biedermeier's elevators during the day (after sunset he was officially restricted, like all men, to the ground floor, although this rule had grown increasingly flexible over the years and, in Stephen's case, was capable of prodigious contortion), could usually count on a moderate number of Christmas tips, being moderately popular himself. He was roundly loathed for a few days every spring around Moving Day, when he charged eye-wateringly exorbitant rates for residents to borrow hand trolleys and use the service elevator for their trunks, but this antipathy was usually exhausted, together with his remaining profits, by August.

If in a particular year Stephen felt that he could stand something a little in excess of moderation, he might make himself available after his official Biedermeier shift ended to deliver packages, pick up dry cleaning, or run downtown to buy cheap cigarettes. When this strategy failed, as it often did, he usually found an excuse to visit the third-floor room of his closest ally, Lucianne. She could scarcely ever be counted on to come through in affairs of the wallet, but her ungenerosity was so predictable as to be steadying—and still better, she was willing to lavish attention on him whenever he complained, which to Stephen was almost as necessary as money. True, Lucianne was no great consoler of persons, but while this prevented most from turning to her in a period of crisis, it posed no problem at all for Stephen. He did not need sympathy, for he always maintained great reserves of that quality for himself. So long as Lucianne was willing to provide him with the appearance of attention, he could supply the appropriate furnishing of pity, concern, indignation, or approval, as the situation required, and she could criticize or laugh at him as much as she liked, so long as she did so as an accompanist, and her counterpoint did not interfere with the pace, nor exceed the volume, of his own part.

"Lucianne," he said in a studiously casual tone, appearing without preamble in her open doorway, "I'm sick of all this nickel-and-dime stuff. I want paper money. You can't do anything without it, but nobody in this blessed building wants a taxi, or tickets anyplace, or their hats blocked. This place has got the most incredible group of unsociable, standoffish shut-ins under heaven. What this hotel needs, if you'll forgive my saying so, is housewives."

"*Te absolvo,*" Lucianne said without looking up from her writing table. All the rooms at the Biedermeier came appointed with ordinary pale resinated chipboard desks, as well as camp beds, washstands, and dressers of similarly dispiriting and characterless origin, but Lucianne had a taste for the light, mobile, and highly worked. She had also demonstrated an early knack for cultivating the affection of her paternal grandmother, a house-proud and cunning old woman whose taste ran along similar lines, and who liked to reward initiative among her offspring and their children. Maria Cecilia often dispensed living bequests to her special pets at whimsical moments, as a reward for their successful court and as a spur to those currently out of favor. She took the Cain-and-Abel approach to family, respecting some offerings and not others, seemingly at random and without ever justifying herself.

She had been a Taliaferro before her marriage into the Caruso family and quite naturally considered the alliance an act of condescension on her people's part. She considered Virginia superior to Delaware and before that, the serene Republic of Venice to the Waldensian valleys of the Piedmont, Protestant Italians being indistinguishable from the Swiss by her reckoning. And she had praised Lucianne at her younger sister Giuliana's expense often enough, calling the former *La Veneziana* when she was in looks and the latter *La Svizzera* whenever she was cross or disheveled or disagreeable, which she was quite often during visits to Maria Cecilia's house.

This all amounted to the present effect that—Maria Cecilia still living, and still with her own home in splendid rig—Lucianne was the sole possessor of several pieces of excellent, scrupulously maintained ladies' furnishings of the Louis XV period, in the Second Style. The two sisters were nevertheless cheerfully inseparable, and as there were plenty of other relatives who liked them both equally, or even preferred the younger, Lucianne's advantage in furniture was outweighed by Giuliana's in china service. Lucianne's writing table belonged to that amiable and convenient little class known as *meuble volant*, or traveling furniture, graceful and slender cabinets, desks, and *bonheurs du jour*, which were never stood against a wall and left stationary, but which could be picked up and carried about the room in pursuit of the best light throughout the day. She kept hers in the middle of the room, where its elaborate nest of open shelves outlined in chased bronze could be admired from all angles. At present most of it was covered in refill paper, heavily marked in her densely spaced longhand and seemingly arranged at random.

"Why housewives? Aren't there enough of them generally?"

"Plenty," Stephen agreed readily. "But they always need something doing. They have lots to do and they can't get it all done themselves. They require a fleet of newspaper boys, milkmen, and odd-jobbers in order to stay in business. Housewives always need another quart of milk or laundry detergent, or someone to look at an appliance or mess about with the doorbell or the pipes or something. I'm sure I could be essential to a building full of housewives. . . ."

"Of course you could, darling," Lucianne said. "If anyone had a doorbell that needed watching, they'd send for you right away. I'm only sorry my household is too small for proper service. But once my bed is made and my bureau straightened, I want for nothing."

"I could get you a pack of cigarettes," Stephen said, although he knew there was no point in the suggestion. Lucianne was never whimsical when she needed something.

"The Lord provides, laddie," she said. "God will see to it that there is a lamb for the burnt offering. When I want a cigarette, I find a man who will give me one. And if I can't find a man to do it, I don't deserve one, that's all. If I ever start carrying my own cigarettes, you'll know things have gotten dangerous for me. You might give me one now, you know."

Stephen, who was more than willing to procure a pack for anyone with a quarter and a preferred brand, did not care to break up his private collection for love or money. But he did so now, as a gesture of respect.

"Everybody's got to have a code," he said, lighting two and handing one over to Lucianne, who took it without acknowledgment and went back to her work. "You stick to yours. The most I could get out of anyone this morning was Pauline saying she'd take an issue of *Forverts* if I could pick one up this evening. But then she found a copy someone left behind on the subway on her way home, so I might as well just have worked all day for all the good it did me."

"That's not a bad idea, you know," Lucianne said. "You could start a resale business. Every evening after rush hour you could comb the trains for cast-off newspapers, and every morning you could peddle them here for a nickel. News probably improves with age, like cheese."

"It should, shouldn't it?" said Stephen. "I wonder why nobody's tried something of the sort before. Yesterday's news is pretty recent for all that, when you think about it. The weather and the stocks might not be worth much a day late, but just about everything else is still useful. You always see bakeries selling yesterday's bread for half price. Why not the paper?"

Lucianne did not answer, but continued writing in her black appointment book, which rested atop the stack of pages on her desk. Stephen waited a minute longer, nettled at being ignored over an idea he considered rather inventive, having already forgotten it was not his to begin with, before sitting cross-legged at Lucianne's feet, looking up at her in fond irritation through the scrollwork.

"I don't like those slippers," he said. "Shearling should never be dyed. Come to think of it, I don't like house slippers for you at all, dyed or virgin wool."

"They're marabou," she said.

"But I like everything else you've got on," he said by way of apology. Lucianne wore a short-waisted, reversible gabardine jacket in hunter green over a pair of camel-colored wool trousers. The outfit suited her enormously but, it must be admitted, had no business being worn with marabou slippers, not even in the privacy of her own room. "And it's only that I hold you to a higher standard than most that makes me so bold as to criticize your shoes."

After another minute without a response, he arranged his features into a frantic, beseeching, Jerry Lewis–type expression.

"Don't make that face at *me*," Lucianne said.

"In his most hilarious role yet," Stephen said, without uncrossing his eyes, "the biggest goof-up who *ever* went to war . . ."

"Come to think of it, he's always playing a bellhop, isn't he?"

"I'm sure I don't know what you mean." Stephen was all dignity and straight lines now, even his eyes.

"I mean, he played one in *The Bellboy*. And then there was *The Errand Boy*. And he was a bellboy again in *The Patsy* just last year, wasn't it?"

"A *bell*boy," Stephen went on, "or as you so aptly put it, a bell*hop*, is a little jack-in-the-box attached to a front desk. He jumps to attention at the first tramp or vagrant who rings a bell. Anyone who can ring a bell is his employer and can use him as they see fit. He bows and opens doors and says 'Yes, sir' and 'No, ma'am' and 'Right away, boss' and parks cars and does whatever else needs doing. Hand me that ash-tray, I need it—thanks. An *elevator* operator operates an elevator, or multiple elevators, as the case may be. I say he *operates* it, because an elevator—and I do not speak here of your modern automated button-bashing affairs, which require no more skill than ringing a bell for a bellboy—is a highly technical piece of machinery." The Biedermeier had three elevator banks, two reasonably active ones dedicated for residents and another for freight, which no one had used in six months.

"Your operator," he continued, "must monitor the an-nunciator board, which in this case has almost certainly not been serviced since it was installed in 1933 and clicks at odd intervals." By now both Stephen and Lucianne were cheerfully ignoring one another, he enjoying his flight of indignation and she her calculations without interference. "He is the captain of a five-by-four vessel, which might drop into the basement if not properly attended to, and which is lined with the most ancient red plush, making the elevator look like a cross between a coffin and a bordello. It is also impossible to clean and retains the scent of every perfume worn and every cigarette smoked within for at least seven years, and it is where certain people like to deposit wads of gum. He must open the right circuit panels at the precise moment, close the doors and scissor gate without a clang, start the motor softly, spin it forward while minding the cables, and prepare the brakes for a soft landing at least five floors before their ultimate destination, because the Biedermeier's elevators are not self-leveling, which means that anyone traveling a shorter distance is likely to be thrown into the ceiling. An elevator operator is more like an engineer than a bellhop. Part pilot and part priest, because the manual elevator also functions as a confessional box, Lucianne—"

"You've never been in a confessional," Lucianne said. "And you wear the same funny little hat as a bellhop."

"We wear entirely different funny little hats," Stephen said, in what was only half mock outrage. "The hat of a bellhop lacks dignity. He must wear a strap under the chin, which makes him look like a child's toy. The hat of an elevator man has no strap. It bears its own weight without restriction, and rests freely on our heads, where, if anything, it makes us look like French legionnaires."

"If I promise to keep that in mind, will you run along now, like a good boy?" Lucianne said. "I've got acres left to do here, and I can't keep track of more than two numbers in my head with a lecture on hats going."

"You might have agreed with me when I said the hat makes me look like a French legionnaire." It did not, quite, but Stephen nonetheless wore the uniform and hat as becomingly as it was possible to do; he was still young enough that anachronism suited him very well. It was a quiet dove gray with a chartreuse lining, blessedly free from piping and epaulets and all other faux military embellishments that so often mar the elevator operator's costume.

"Stephen," Lucianne said, putting down her pen at last and regarding him seriously, "if I were to give you a dollar for your very own, would you go away and come back again in about a month, when I can cope with you?"

"Is it a bill?" Stephen asked. "Because I won't move for a silver dollar. I haven't got room for any more coins in my pockets. They're insufficient to my needs and they make me sound like a piggy bank when I walk."

He left the room in muffled, jingling dignity, also taking the ashtray with him. A few hours later, when they passed one another without speaking in the hall, he noticed with pleasure that she had changed into a very shabby, very becoming pair of velvet loafers.

THE HANGING OF
THE GREENS

Chapter Two

Ordinarily Lucianne required neither time nor leisure to deal with Stephen's company, not even
when he ventured to criticize her clothing. She
appreciated the flow of steady nonsense that accompanied
him as a cloud by day and a pillar of fire by night, and could
tune it either in or out as she liked without effort or incon-
venience. But for a great work of this kind, Stephen was no
fit helpmeet. Lucianne was scarcely fit for it herself, having
very little head for numbers, but she was willing to make an
exception for money.

She was willing to make an exception for the *making*

of money, rather, since Lucianne had a habit of ignoring numbers whenever her spending outpaced her income. In such periods she preferred to take refuge in vague bafflement, and over time realized it was possible to cultivate incompetence, where none had previously existed, through the sheer persistent application of her willpower toward a failure in her understanding. She was determined not to understand loss in detail; all she needed to know was whether or not she was behind in some category or other, at which point she consigned it to a profound mental vacancy, until such time as the problem either corrected itself or failed catastrophically, which to Lucianne amounted to much the same thing. At the point of catastrophe she would forget about it permanently, if it could be forgotten without great consequence, or else send her grandmother a tactful, chatty letter, which almost always resulted in a contribution toward her upkeep. On the rare occasions when Maria Cecilia failed to kick in, Lucianne would either pawn one of her lesser bequests or beg one of her editors to let her write the sort of society column she could afford to despise in seasons of affluence.

But today Lucianne could afford to despise anything or anybody as much as she pleased, and she very merrily damned all aged relatives, pawnbrokers, aspiring hostesses, bill collectors, and newspaper editors as she tallied her figures. It was tiring but gratifying work; counting money as it came in was a very different undertaking to counting money as it went out, and Lucianne had been making money frequently, consistently, and with tremendous relish for more than two months now. And she was in love, or something very near it, which far from making her indifferent to money, had instead sharpened her appreciation and avidity for it.

Before this sudden change in fortune, things had been very much the reverse with her. In August she had been cut loose from the last of her society-page reporting after submitting a mean-spirited and comic review of *Career Girl, Watch Your Step!*, a book that purported to advise "every young woman who lives in a city, or is planning to move to one." It was an absurd, badly written book, hurriedly and ineptly published, and its author's only claim to competence was that his daughter had been one of the victims in the previous year's Career Girls Murders. The advice found in *Watch Your Step* ran along fairly unimaginative fatherly lines: "Avoid the beatnik fringe element. . . . Don't think of yourself as being safe. Think of yourself as being in danger all the time. . . . The city is not a safe place." The book was self-serious, plodding, impractical, exaggerated, and frightened of its own shadow; the picture on the dust jacket displayed the author brandishing a pistol, and he further recommended that all females wishing to move to New York City should take up residence at the YWCA. He had the twin protections of convention and outrage on his side, for books preaching timidity and spiritlessness to young women were always popular, and seemingly no one was willing to read a bereaved father with anything like a critical eye. The spirit of provocation was supereminent in Lucianne, and she could not resist such a temptation. In most circumstances she was socially shrewd and interested in consensus, but the more that a given subject was guarded from teasing, the more strongly did she feel the perverse impulse rise within her. There had besides been in the past few years a publishing mania for books advising single women living alone; brisk, tasteless, overbearing, too familiar by half, forever positioning themselves as the only honest friend a girl had. They might vary in tone or licentiousness, but whether they thought that their reader ought to sleep around or remain chaste, all of them recommended diets, regimented living, and little sample budgets of one's monthly income, and offered lessons on talking to men as if to bright children, such that Lucianne had a wealth of accumulated resentments and pet annoyances to spend on this latest example. She was eloquent and occasionally inspired on the subject, hating in particular the chipper tone of the suggested budgets. Lucianne was opposed to budgeting in principle. She spent money freely and unthinkingly until she suddenly ran out, at which point she quietly panicked until the crisis passed, and considered that the only relationship with money a self-respecting and dignified person could possibly have.

The double murder had received more than a year of sustained and sensational attention, in part due to its shocking violence and the parade of suspects, which included at least one retracted confession, but also due to the frequently repeated claim that both girls belonged to "distinguished" families, which had offended Lucianne both as a reporter and as a member of good society. The victims had been described as beauties and as being from the best families; to Lucianne's quick and assessing eye they were clearly neither, and she resented the exaggeration. Lucianne pitied anyone murdered in her bed, but further than that, she was not willing to go. No Midwestern professionals, however competent, could be considered prominent in any honest assessment, and besides which, social elevation seemed to her like an insultingly poor exchange for a murdered child.

Lucianne had not formally submitted her review in the usual way for an article intended for publication. She had left only a few—very few—mimeographed copies on the desks of some particular friends who shared her sense of humor, who might appreciate something scathing as a necessary corrective to the scourge of favorable coverage.

But those copies had not remained very few; they began to circulate across a widening network of less-discriminating desks, and what had in private appeared to be ferocious yet discerning, clear-eyed and waggish, somehow now looked mean-spirited, grubby, and "not in good taste." Very quickly the office's collective opinion moved against her. No one who may have laughed in private would admit to it now; no one offered either concession or justification on her behalf. All lips were pursed and hearts were shut against her.

Lucianne, who so often enjoyed the pleasant, hazy comfort of being part of a consensus, was never more disobliging or contrary than when she knew herself to be under siege. After the first seasick moments of a dawning realization that her joke hadn't gone over, she denied mortification further purchase in her mind and grew belligerent. If opinions in the newsroom had been split, she might have been hectored into at least the appearance of contrition, and certainly would have made a very graceful apology. Lucianne had a talent for apologizing beautifully—her apologies were frank, womanly, sincere, and unguarded—and had in this way often won enemies to her side who would never have appreciated her in moments of triumph. But she won no one to her side that day, only grew more justified in her own opinion and less coherent in expressing it. By the time she had been called into her editor's office for a closed-door meeting, she was nearly weeping with anger. The tears made her look conscious of guilt, which made her angrier still. If it had only been brought up in a different moment, on an occasion where hilarity and irreverence had prevailed, in a lavish hour after lunch instead of in the abstemious midmorning, when eyes were sober, stomachs unfortified, and humor wholly absent.

She would not apologize for what she had written, nor for the style in which she had written it. Neither would she apologize for her unlicensed use of the mimeograph machine; practically everyone did the same from time to time, and besides, if her editors had *liked* the piece, if they had laughed rather than chosen to take offense (for Lucianne did not even at this point believe that anyone could have been really disturbed by her review, that they only pretended to do so for indistinct, priggish reasons), then even if they had not seen fit to publish it, they would not have minded her making copies. It was only an add-on, an ancillary charge to make sure the first one would stick. It would be contemptible, at this point, to disown the cruelty of what she had written in order to be liked or forgiven. Occasional cruelty, at least when it was leavened with clear and intelligent judgment, was nothing to be ashamed of, particularly when the writer in question had warmth and pluck to back it. Certainly it was preferable—infinitely preferable—to the morose and dampening cruelty of this unified sanctimony. Sentiment without spirit, weakness without tenderness—that was the problem with them! That final meeting had grown into an informal tribunal, and finally saw six editors and subeditors all mobilized against her, as determined to extract an expression of shame from her as a dentist pulling a rotten tooth. But in addition to rejecting the moral force of their disapproval, Lucianne now denied their jurisdiction over her writing, uncommissioned, unsanctioned, and unedited as it had been. If they hated it enough to end her already-tenuous working relationship with the paper, they needed to have no part in it. She offered to repay the copy clerk the thirty cents that using the mimeograph machine would have cost them, but the offer was rejected. She subsequently left the building with an air of beleaguered virtue and all the force of her original opinion intact, although with little else. No promise of future work, no likelihood of any future recommendation when indignation had finally died down, no salvageable professional contacts. There had not even been time to collect her latest portfolio of clippings, and certainly no one who would be willing to forward them to her at the hotel; she might never have written for a newspaper in her life, for all that she had to show for it.

"And all that—six grown men with better things to do lined up in a single cramped office just to scold me, for a silly little joke," she wrote to Giuliana in her next weekly letter, sent this time significantly later than usual. It had taken several days of rehearsal and a curious, anxious mental blankness before she could allow herself to tell the story of what had happened to anyone else; she was not willing to sacrifice the comic element at the heart of it, and was determined that whosoever heard about it next from *her* was at least going to laugh. "Although it *was* a good joke, and even rather nicely put in a few places—but they were determined not to enjoy themselves. You know how it is, when people decide to punish you for laughing when they think you shouldn't. It's remarkable how much otherwise really intelligent people seem to hate laughter, how much in the way of taste and sense they're willing to sacrifice at the altar of their miserable, false, lying, discourteous politeness."

So much for the newspaper trade! Which was falling apart at the moment anyways, and had been for some time. Where was the *New York Daily Mirror*? Where was the *World-Telegram and The Sun*? Where was the *Journal-American*? Dying, consolidated, dead. It had been a blessing, and not even in disguise. Lucianne was lucky to be alive, and to be shot of the whole field while she was still young. She had been shot of a number of fields while younger still—the telephone company, the insurance business, stenotypy—and it had always been lucky for her to have left, in the end. But there was in the meantime the question of what to do about money. Lucianne could usually get hold of modest sums here and there without too much trouble, but quite a few deaths still stood in the way between herself and real, working capital, and what Lucianne wanted was not a gift, not an advance, but a steady and predictable income, one that would not dry up nor change course unexpectedly, but remain exactly where and how she left it.

For although Lucianne had paid a very reasonable rent (and sometimes paid significantly less than her reasonable rent) to the Biedermeier for the better part of a decade, she did not live cheaply. By far her greatest expense was her clubs, and she would not give them up for anything. She belonged to far too many, declined to sit on any of their miscellaneous boards, plan parties, or raise funds—and they were all of them in fundraising season three or even four times a year—or to behave in any way that might demonstrate either usefulness or civic-mindedness. But she never fell behind on her dues, and she would never surrender her membership to any of them. Lucianne was a gentleman on the subject. She might default on her bills, contribute short rent in months of idleness, and make off with ink ribbons and memorandum pads during bouts of employment, but her club dues were always paid in scrupulous readiness and in full. Her eighteenth birthday had marked her exit from junior membership in the Social Register and she now paid the full annual subscription price, plus another $8.50 for the Visiting Index; there were also the Colonial Dames, the Daughters of the American Revolution, and the Woman's Club of Newport, at home in Delaware. In New York she also belonged to the Colony Club, the Women's National Republican Club, the Huguenot Society, the Women's Press Club, and the Sweet Briar College Club, although at no time during her eighteen months of enrollment had she been in any danger of graduating. She could not have done without any of them. The Colony Club's interiors had been designed by Lady Mendl, whose standards for architectural harmony Lucianne positively worshipped. The Huguenots' library was unparalleled, the Republicans' chef excellent, and the Women's Press Club possessed furniture nearly as exquisitely maintained as Lucianne's own, including a blue-and-ivory Dagestan rug, hand-painted five o'clock tea tables of astonishing delicacy, and a Persian loving cup mounted over the fireplace. Impossible to yield!

To drop either the Register or the DAR would be, if not a stain, certainly a smudge on the family escutcheon, to say nothing of the loss of the hours of pleasure she and Giuliana frequently found looking up old school friends in "Married

Maidens." Together they would decipher the degree of blessedness enjoyed by each in their exalted state according to the enigmatic series of letters following their names. This consoling and familiar string of gibberish indicated to those in the know one's clubs, old school ties, fraternities, sororities, and memberships in various professional and charitable societies, such that Lucianne and Giuliana might whistle in pitying contempt over "Amory, Maud . . . Spalding," where Spalding had contributed no more than a mere Bow.Rp. (Bowdoin graduate, Republican) to her Jl.Myf.Cda.Rh.Tf.Ss.Dv. (Junior League, *Mayflower* Descendants, Colonial Dames of America, Rockaway Hunt, Turf & Field, Southern Society, *Deutscher Verein*), or raise an eyebrow at the shocking good fortune of "Sturgis, Olivia . . . Armsbee," whose name as an unmarried maiden had appeared nowhere in those battered black-and-pumpkin volumes. Lucianne's own name had been published in twenty-eight volumes, respectably followed by Wk.Ht.Dar.Cth.Cd.R.Cly. (Westminster Kennel, Huguenot Society, Daughters of the American Revolution, Catholic, Colonial Dames, Racquet & Tennis, Colony Club). Girls who had married or been nominated into the Register might come or go as they pleased, but Lucianne had been born within the pages of the book, and she would not depart from them while there was breath in her body and twelve dollars to be found somewhere in the world.

That is not to say that she took the Register at all seriously; it was merely sacred to her. In fact, it was largely thanks to the Register that Lucianne was now working so mightily to cope with such a torrent of sums. She had spent the rest of August and the better part of September in perfect idleness, usually as a guest in somebody or other's weekend home or boating party. As October neared, even those sporadic attempts at economy failed her, and she began unwillingly to consider the prospect of once again seeking employment, when of all people Mrs. Mossler gave her a perfect alternative.

That afternoon she had been part of a little group of Biedermeier residents crowded around Mrs. Mossler's office door, which also included the residential manager, Katherine Heap, whom Lucianne thought of as something better than a nuisance but less than a friend, and Pauline Carter, who lived on the second floor and was socially unsalvageable. Pauline was at least good-looking, and very stylish, too, and as her particular style tended to complement Lucianne's own, Lucianne had no trouble cultivating a friendly, unscrupulous attitude toward her. On this occasion, Pauline's black-and-white racer-back dress was nearly as abbreviated as her hair, which she always wore closely cropped and just barely curled. Mrs. Mossler's seafoam drop-waist dress might have been from just this last season, or a faithfully preserved original, revived after a thirty-year dormancy. Katherine's clothes did not bear thinking about, so Lucianne did her civil best to forget them.

They had been discussing the New York World's Fair, both in its present guise, which most of them had visited at least once, and the 1939 exposition, which only Mrs. Mossler remembered, although both had taken place on the same grounds in Queens. In fact, quite a few of the pavilions and cutting-edge exhibition halls from 1939 were being repurposed for some of the 1964 fair's less-than-cutting-edge needs, and the second version seemed well on track to lose the city almost as much money as the first had. While it was still in the process of failing, however, the organizers had contracted the Pinkerton Agency for hundreds of security guards to maintain the grounds and watch the pavilions until the fair reopened in the spring.

Like Lucianne, Pauline had recently fallen out from the bottom of the journalism trade, although Lucianne had written society columns for newspapers like the *Journal-American* and trade articles for *The American Home* and *Field & Stream*, and Pauline had worked as a typesetter for a lot of little foreign, Mickey Mouse concerns downtown, each with self-important names like *The Italian Alarm* or *The People's Voice Is a Fist*. Unlike Lucianne, Pauline seemed to enjoy living cheaply or at least within her means, but she was also responsible for supporting her paternal grandparents, Judith and Clarence Carter. They had raised her from infancy with tremendous affection and had made almost no provisions for their old age, so losing even this relatively small income had made finding work a matter of real urgency for her. Typesetting of the hot-metal type, in which Pauline had been trained, was sweaty, awkward work, and not many places called for it, but it was nevertheless with real misery and profound shame that she had shared the news of her latest hire with her fellow residents.

"The World's Fair would be bad enough," she said, twisting the hiring pamphlet in her hands. "If Judith knew I'd had anything to do with a project of Robert Moses's, she'd never speak to me again. And she'd be right not to."

"He's nothing to get worked up over," Lucianne said. "It's not his fault that everybody in the city needs highways to drive on but that nobody wants him to build them anywhere." She had spent much of the previous summer forwarding questions to his office over a piece on the city's zoning history and found him to be a slightly tired-seeming, unaffected man, one she rather liked despite herself.

"Even you can't really like him," Pauline said.

"Have it your way," Lucianne said, refusing to get worked up herself. "He can go up against the wall with the others."

"But it's really the Pinkertons I don't know what to do about," Pauline said.

"I thought the Pinkertons went out with the first Red Scare," said Katherine. "Are they really still a going concern?"

"They abide," said Pauline darkly. "They abide, even though they don't have nearly as many railroad workers to hit on the head these days. They're mostly in the protection racket now. Take a look at this," and she thrust the crumpled leaflet into Katherine's hands. It read:

PEACE THROUGH UNDERSTANDING
Guarding the 1964–1965 NEW YORK
WORLD'S FAIR against
BURGLARS, PICKPOCKETS,
RIOTERS, VANDALS,
DISHONEST EMPLOYEES,
AND UNRULY DRUNKS
PINKERTON'S INC.
"THE EYE THAT NEVER SLEEPS"
Inquire at Pinkerton Security Building
at Flushing Meadows Corona Park.

Below this was a cartoon of several bright, uniformed young people posed in the act of picking up litter and returning a purse to a grateful old woman.

"Oh, Pauline," said Lucianne in real sympathy. "Those are all your favorite sort of people."

"At least I'm only a matron," Pauline said, although it was impossible to associate the word *matron* with anything to do with Pauline. "We can't all be cops, I mean. They put me with the Lost Children's Bureau, and the uniform comes complete with a truly awful khaki sash. I think the idea is to make us look like park rangers, so we don't frighten the children. That part's not so bad. We're posted in a little cottage; people bring in stray kids, and it's my job to try to find out if they know their parents' names or address or anything at all. Most of them don't. 'Daddy's called Hector and we live in a red house. He's very tall' is usually the best they can do before they start crying. Then we give them butter-and-jam sandwiches and let them color with crayons for a while, which usually cheers them up, and eventually somebody comes for them—which is a good thing, too, because everybody clears out for the night except for one of the monsignors at the Vatican pavilion. I don't know why, but somebody's always camped out there overnight. Is that customary, do you know?" This was directed at Lucianne.

"Do they celebrate Mass there?"

Pauline shook her head. "I don't know." She had been raised in beautiful ignorance of every faith, although her grandparents, committed atheists each, had failed to inculcate in her their own antipathy toward religion; she responded to new details about every denomination as though she were hearing of the progress of a beloved, if slightly abnormal, cousin. "How do you know if someone has celebrated Mass?"

"Do they hold church services there? Do people take Communion?"

"Oh yes, I think so. People are always going into the chapel and coming out much later."

"That's it, then. If a priest is celebrating Mass, then someone has to stay with the Blessed Sacrament while it's reposed."

"Oh, I see," said Pauline brightly. She did not understand what this meant even in part, but she could sense Lucianne growing slightly stiff, as if bracing to be insulted. Without quite realizing it, Lucianne mentally included Pauline in the category of Protestants, considering Pauline's Jewish and atheistic background as a sort of Protestantism, and she did not appreciate jokes about her religion from that quarter.

Lucianne was not overly conscientious on the subject of Catholicism—she generally avoided attending St. Patrick's Cathedral—although she retained a proprietary affection for its sacraments and traditions, and in fact she began each week with the vague but settled intention of going to Mass. Yet somehow by Sunday morning she almost always found that her schedule would not permit it, at which point she settled her conscience by intending even more firmly to make up for it by going the next week.

"Well, I think it's very sweet that the Sacrament always has company," Pauline finished lamely, and the conversation grew in danger of floundering before Mrs. Mossler rescued it.

Mrs. Mossler had been particularly enthusiastic about the "new" fair, talking eagerly of the last one, in 1939, when she herself was but newly attached to the Biedermeier and bore far greater responsibility for her residents' entertainment, as well as sharing all she could remember (and she remembered a great deal) of the nations represented, pavilions visited, muralists commissioned, novelties displayed. She remembered with particular interest the pavilion that had exhibited appliances from the American Radiator and Standard Sanitary Corporation, the halls belonging to the National Biscuit Company, the Vermont Maple Tree Sugar Company, a local chauffeuring union—"and that strange little man who took us all to go see it—Ted Pelham, or Palmer, he called himself, though I have no idea what his real name might have been. He'd started a sort of escort guide service a few years before, during the Depression, since there were so many nice men out of work and so many nice women who couldn't go anywhere interesting without them. He called at all the ladies' hotels in those days. I remember he had a little patter for it: 'Suppose I guarantee to have a dozen university men, all in their twenties, with Social Register backgrounds, perfect manners and reputations, well-dressed and thoroughly presentable, ready to squire any woman you have here wherever she wants to go, and prepared to deliver her back home as her own brother would? Suppose I supply the men, can you supply the women?' He ran after all the columnists—he was absolutely mad for publicity, always hanging around the Stork Club trying to get his photograph taken—Lucius Beebe and Cholly Knickerbocker especially. But I don't suppose you girls remember them?"

Only Lucianne did, although she didn't think much of either. She felt that society reporters ought to report for society itself, not for the general public pressing their noses up against the glass.

"Anyhow, he rounded up as many out-of-work Ivy League boys as he could find—they had to be tall, too, I remember, at least five foot ten—steady, no-nonsense. They never drank and they never used hair oil—perfectly well-behaved, nothing at all like taxi dancers, no matter what

CHRISTMAS AT THE WOMEN'S HOTEL

people said. He ran it along the lines of the Post Office, nothing could stay them from the swift completion of their appointed rounds. I hired a few of his young men myself when I wanted to see the fair. None of my men friends could have afforded to take me, you know, although they wouldn't have admitted it for the world. They were all perfectly acceptable young men—except for Ted. One didn't like him; one almost never does, with big-idea types, even when the ideas are good. Endlessly self-promoting, and for all his talk about consoling lonely hearts, it was perfectly clear that he didn't like women at all."

"And they came to the hotel?" Katherine asked, surprised. The chaperonage at the Biedermeier was never strict, running largely on a rather shabby and shopworn honor system since Mrs. Mossler could afford no further inspection, but it was nevertheless pleasantly shocking to imagine the lobby filled with paid escorts in their mothers' generation.

"Oh, yes," Mrs. Mossler said, unconcerned. "It was a perfectly aboveboard operation. You could get away with rather a lot in those days, in the interest of giving men jobs. I don't mean that he was getting away with anything unwholesome, only zany. I can't remember why they arrested him now. I think he must have needed a license and couldn't get one, because it wasn't for anything indecent, I would have remembered that. I don't know why more men don't get up that kind of service now. I suppose because they arrest you. Because there are still quite a lot of places that won't let you in without an escort, although it's nothing like it was then, of course. You really don't know how nice it is to be able to go so many places by yourself." At this point Mrs. Mossler's thoughts drifted back to the fair, and there would be no hope of returning her to any earlier topic: "Oh, and there was the Arctic Girl's tomb of ice. I don't think she was really Arctic, just a girl in a bathing suit who would lie down in a bed of ice as long as she could stand it. Maybe it doesn't sound like much, but everybody wanted to go see a girl being frozen alive in some ice. My, but she looked cold in there. I'm sure they won't have anything like that there now, would they, Pauline?"

"I haven't seen much of the grounds, I'm afraid," Pauline said. "I could tell you a fair amount about the pictures the lost children have drawn for me, but none of them have yet mentioned a bathing beauty Popsicle."

"No, I suppose they wouldn't. It was very entertaining at the time, but it doesn't seem like the sort of thing people want to see nowadays. I was cold myself just from watching her. No, that wasn't anything to do with the escorts. It was at the fair, near Admiral Byrd's Penguin Island, just past the Congress of World's Beauties and Nature's Mistakes. . . ."

But Lucianne was long past listening. She made her apologies in equal parts politeness and haste before retreating to her room to take notes in her address book and make some probing phone calls. There was no point in wasting eligible men on Biedermeier girls, of course, but how many girls did she know who needed a well-bred occasional man, girls who would be more than happy to pay for the introduction, so long as he could be counted on to be punctual and charming? Not someone you were in real danger of liking, who might quarrel with you tomorrow and then leave you without an escort for the rest of the week, but someone steady, impersonal, a good guest who wouldn't embarrass you either at the table or on the dance floor, someone wholly disconnected from one's own life, and whose idea of a good time lined up precisely with yours, because it was almost a certainty that the man you really liked was apt to get drunk at the worst moment, or to take a shine to one of your friends, or to vanish partway through dinner with the other unattached males in search of a better party, whereas the man who considered you his job for the evening had no reason to fail you—and besides, didn't Lucianne know everyone who was worth knowing? People might criticize or even dislike her sense of humor, her arch and unsentimental, pitiless manner, but none of them had ever criticized her taste. If Lucianne said he was all right for an evening, then he was, and that counted for something.

She also drew up an extensive list of rules, many of them underlined more than once, since so many of the principles regulating good behavior went without saying socially, but could always bear repetition in a professional setting:

A GUIDE FOR GUIDES

1. No more than one drink an hour, no more than six drinks a night. Sobriety is essential.
2. Be polite, not personal. Listen to her with interest. Keep your side of the conversation general, but not dull, and don't bring up your private life. By no means ought she to know where you live, who your particular friends are, and *certainly* not the names of any other clients you might happen to see.
3. All contact with a client must be made through the office. Never give a girl your own telephone number. This job is no replacement for a social life of your own.
4. The evening ends at her front door.
5. You may choose to give her the impression rule #4 is slightly burdensome in *her* case—but only slightly, and only an impression. Do not invite her to break it.
6. Any violation of rule #4, however minute, will result in dismissal.

7. Treat her like your own sister. Make sure she has a wonderful time. She could have a perfectly nice time on her own, so if she's paying for the evening's entertainment, it had better be wonderful. If she's on the wall, dance with her; if she's popular, be sure to stay off the wall yourself and be ready for a cheerful reunion at a moment's notice.

8. Return any change from your expenses envelope to the client at the end of the evening. Tip conservatively unless she directs you to do otherwise; it's not your money.

9. Don't haggle, bargain, angle for gifts, or drop hints about tips for yourself. And for heaven's sake, *don't* mention in an offhand way that you've had your eye on this or that watch, cigarette case, python-skin shoes, mother-of-pearl studs, a trip to Bermuda, et cetera. Avoid discussions of your own poverty, no matter how grinding. If you're that hard up, call the office for more appointments, or contact the *New York Times*' Neediest Cases Fund.

If Lucianne had encountered very little trouble convincing her male acquaintances to sign up for the Guide Escorts, she found even less among her women friends. Even girls with steady dates called her up. Deanie Foote wanted a nice young man to accompany her to a traveling performance of Amy Beach's Mass in E-flat by the Handel and Haydn Society, being taxed with a boyfriend who *would* whistle tunelessly along with the orchestra without ever realizing he was doing it. Betty Egerton wanted someone to go with her to St. Thomas Church whenever her grandmother was in town, being engaged to an otherwise extremely good-natured young man who became tiresomely strident on the subject of religion, "as long as he's between five nine and five eleven and has light-brown hair, because Grandmother's eyesight isn't at all good."

———··———

As it happened, Carol Lipscomb and Patricia De Boer (both on the eleventh floor) were hiding something from Mrs. Mossler, although in neither case did money have anything to do with it. It was rather the result of several coincidences that were unusually closely spaced together.

Carol had unexpectedly received a Latin translation exam scholarship, one that came with a certificate and a check for $250. It was a considerable amount—more money than she had ever seen at one time in her life, or likely would again—and it struck fear, caution, prudence, and even Yankee thrift into her soul, which was ordinarily swept attractively clean of all such virtues. She had paid off her back rent at once, replaced her winter shoes and best cloth coat, sent $25 to her youngest brother, and put the rest into Ridgewood Savings Bank.

Patricia came by her windfall in a more usual fashion; an unmarried aunt of hers died and left her a small annuity. Patricia did not believe in either banks or savings, and she reveled in her small-scale brush with wealth, which had no effect on her spirit whatever. It was the little extras that counted with her, the slice of cake to go with her coffee, the filmy scarf bought unhesitatingly and on sight, drinks before dinner, and long, luxurious subway rides, paid for with real, thoroughbred subway tokens, instead of slugs that only worked on the turnstile half the time. And she bought several stone eagles.

Patricia and Lucianne had been brought together several years before in a concerted local attempt to halt the Penn Station demolition. Both of them were particularly attached to the building, Lucianne because she loved pink granite and anything in the Beaux Arts line, and Patricia because, while she detested Beaux Arts and thought modeling a civic building after a bank was psychologically destructive, did not trust the city to replace it with anything better. The movement nevertheless failed, despite Lucianne's letter-writing campaigns and Patricia's brief, fumbled attempt to chain herself to a moving platform, and demolition began in 1963.

But demolition progressed as slowly as all other municipal undertakings in New York, which gave citizens plenty of time to make off with as many of the grand ornaments that had once adorned the building as they possibly could. There had been twenty-two stone sculptures of eagles on Old Penn Station's facade, colossal-headed and imposing. Fourteen of them were too big for personal use and had to be carted away piecemeal; many of these eventually turned up at naval academies and farming colleges, a small group of lightly irrigated college boys being ideal stewards and finding the carrying away of heavy, historically significant objects completely irresistible after the sixth or seventh drink of an evening.

But eight of the eagles were relatively small, weighing only two or three hundred pounds apiece, and could conceivably be brought up the freight elevator of a women's hotel, even a freight elevator whose maintenance had been slightly neglected for the past decade, provided one knew the sort of person who abstracted sculptures out of city demolition projects at night. Patricia knew many such persons, and had the money not only to incentivize them to bring the eagles to her, but also to encourage Stephen to take an impromptu sick day, dropping the key to the freight elevator on the carpet outside her door before he did so.

Carol had at first approved the project—she always supported Patricia's art, even and especially when she did not like it—but as the year lengthened and the eagles stared at her every night with those penetrating, sightless stone eyes that seemed to follow one even in sleep, she became paranoid, and took to locking their door, even pretending not to be at home whenever Mrs. Mossler tried to stop by.

Mrs. Mossler did not for a moment suspect the girls of harboring eagles—certainly a victimless crime, if it was a crime at all, since they were supposed to have been demolished—although she did on occasion worry that they might have had something to do with the recent break-in at the American Museum of Natural History. Mrs. Mossler, being an innocent on the details of crime, as she was innocent of so many details of life, could conceive of nothing worse, nor more particular, than one of her girls "having something to do with" one. There had been so many jewels stolen, and only ten recovered. . . .

But she could not politely ask them if they were harboring stolen jewels, or jewel thieves for that matter. To put her mind at ease, she decided that they probably were harboring stolen jewels. This relaxed her, because it meant she could stop worrying about whether they were harboring stolen jewels, and could focus her energies on protecting them from the consequences, should the need ever arise.

"They're going to fall through the floor one of these days," Carol warned Patricia after a particularly restless night. "You've got to start thinking about getting them out of here. They can't stay here forever. Just imagine if they plummeted through every single ceiling between here and the first floor."

"I don't think there's anybody I especially like just below us," Patricia said after a moment's reflection. "No, not on any of the floors. Everybody I like is on the western side of the hotel."

———··———

It was lucky for Josephine Marbury that Patricia liked her and that she subsequently lived out of range of the eagles on the second floor's western wing. She was, in fact, the closest thing the Biedermeier had to a genuine jewel thief, having taken to occasional gallant bouts of pickpocketing after the hotel had suspended breakfast service. This loss had not reduced everyone in the building to the same pitch of desperation, but Josephine had already stretched her small and mercilessly fixed income to the very limit, and she was terrified both of going hungry and of being put into a home. The two prospects had in fact become curiously linked in her mind, so that whenever she felt the lash of the first, she grew more frightened of the possibility of the second. Her thefts were modest, covert, and for the most part deniable; she was sometimes ashamed and quite often proud of them. She was at least looking after herself.

There was nothing in her background that might have bespoken a career as a pickpocket. She had been for many years a newspaperwoman and a caricaturist, and had been particularly in demand as the latter after 1934, when her nearest competition, Peggy Bacon, lost her stomach for it and started illustrating books instead. But it had been some time since anything of Josephine's style had been called for among her remaining contacts—and besides which, people no longer seemed to have the faces that cried out for caricature nowadays. All the well-known faces *now* were brisk, friendly, well-fed, and well-groomed. This was perfectly all right for their owners but useless for a sketch artist. Where were the grand noses, the majestic, massive heads so sunk in patrician dignity as to be nearly eyeless, the chinless and goitered necks of her own youth? So now she only drew on a friendly basis and on request, and in the meanwhile had managed to restore herself to a tolerable, modest splendor of the studio-apartment type through the judicious introduction of occasional theft.

She was quite short, only an inch over five feet, and slight, but no longer overly thin, as she had been last summer. She wore her good, old-fashioned serge suits with real dash, having them tailored every two or three years to remain within hailing distance of the dictates of fashion. Her hair she wore in the same severe, short bob of 1927, only by now some of the fire had gone out of it and the auburn was matched with pearl. She looked smart, but not too smart, and could disappear into a crowd without much effort.

It was only Pauline who found her out, which did not trouble Josephine much, although on principle she was embarrassed to have been seen. But Pauline was an anarchist, or at least had been raised by anarchists, and was herself embarrassed to have noticed anything at all. She would not have noticed, except that her new job was in Flushing Meadows Park, which meant instead of walking downtown in the early morning, she now walked a few blocks uptown to catch the 7 train. It was on this walk one day in early autumn that she had seen Josephine very neatly detach a few dollar bills from a pocketbook belonging to a woman so laden with shopping bags she could scarcely see.

It had not been possible to walk on without being seen herself, and they'd had to acknowledge one another. Josephine was conscious in an instant of Pauline having caught her in the act, and spent the rest of the day in mortal dread of being lectured or worse, advised by a good-looking young person, one with a job, with friends and prospects and every expectation of future security.

It had not been quite as bad as she had feared; Pauline had only reappeared to knock on Josephine's door later that evening and right away said, "I'm very sorry if seeing me was at all upsetting this morning. I hope you know I don't pry into other people's business, and I don't pretend to know things when I don't."

Now that she was no longer required to defend herself, Josephine was happy, even grateful, to talk to Pauline about it. Without quite deciding to confide in her, maintaining an instinctive and self-preserving state of wariness, Josephine could acknowledge that things were mighty dear these days, that an income didn't mean what it used to mean, and that it was easy, terribly easy, for someone no longer young and productive to get swept up into the machinery that seemed to spring up around old people for the purpose of breaking them back down into their constituent parts.

Pauline agreed with real warmth, but did not take advantage of her position by talking politics or presuming to advise Josephine on how to stretch a penny.

She could not, however, resist the urge to say, "I do hope you'll be careful," although she realized at once that this had been a mistake, for Josephine's sweet old face stiffened into a hostile, wolfish expression.

"What a very good idea that is," Josephine said. "Thank you for the suggestion. I'll be sure to consider it."

"I'm terribly sorry, Josephine," Pauline said. "That was all wrong—it's not what I meant to say at all."

The wolfish look receded, and Josephine remained

perfectly polite—even a shade kindlier than polite—but whatever possibility there had been of speaking frankly together had vanished, and Pauline soon wished her a good night and left the room.

———··———

Mrs. Mossler stood nervously outside the door to Patricia and Carol's room, debating with herself. On the one hand, no one had been hurt as a result of the museum break-in. On the other hand, a museum was something like a school or a church and ought to be treated with a little reverence.

She raised a hand to knock, and just as quickly lowered it. Suppose they were hiding stolen jewels in their room. Just what did she propose to do about it? She could encourage them to return them to the museum quietly, without drawing attention to themselves. She could warn them of the danger they were risking. But no option presented itself to her that did not sound ridiculous, and finally when she steeled herself to knock and Patricia answered the door, looking innocent as the dawn, she could not bring herself to say anything but "Hello, Pat. Did you know the men who broke into the Hall of Gems used an ordinary glass cutter?"

"I don't know that I did," Patricia said, not holding the door open any wider than was absolutely necessary. "Although I suppose it stands to reason they would. There weren't any guards on duty, I remember reading."

Mrs. Mossler considered this almost as good as a confession. At this point, she decided the best thing would be for her to know nothing, and carefully trained her eyes on Patricia's face, without looking any further into the room. "Well, that's all I came to say, really. . . . I do hope you'll look after yourselves, Pat. It's very easy for things to build up, don't you think?"

"I suppose so," Patricia said, puzzled. "You look after yourself, too." After closing the door, she turned thoughtfully to Carol and said, "I think Mrs. Mossler knows we've been stealing her paper."

———··———

Unusually this year, Katherine waited until the second Sunday in Advent to attend to the hanging of the greens in her bedroom. This undertaking properly belonged to the first Sunday in Advent, but as that day had fallen in late November this year, Katherine had declined to observe it. She had deliberately convinced herself the night before that she felt a cold coming on, one that would require urgent cosseting, and dedicated the whole of that Sunday morning to making herself queenly comfortable in bed. This meant wearing her warmest bed jacket with scalloped sleeves, drinking strong coffee out of a squat old china caudle cup, eating an orange, arranging a slice each of ham and coffee cake on a tray, and reading the second volume of *Kristin Lavransdatter*.

A Sunday spent in bed had to be managed with a firm hand. Well-planned and properly arranged, it could be restorative and wholesome, gladdening the spirit and brightening the complexion. But an impromptu Sunday in bed, wearing haphazard and mismatched bedclothes, with hair unwashed and crumbs in the pillowcase, with the crossword spoiled and no plans settled for the evening, was little better than a torment.

Katherine always arranged her creaturely comforts with a surer hand in the winter. In spring and summer, whenever day outpaced the night wit, she declined in both confidence and poise. There was so much clock time left in each summer afternoon that it exceeded her best judgment well before sunset. She dithered, she hesitated, she wavered; she would invariably order the wrong thing at lunch, begin reading books she knew she would never finish, pick quarrels with Lucianne, avoid Arthur, her sponsor in AA, and creep out of meetings early; she made ill-judged purchases and threw away necessary, even beautiful things in fits of misguided certainty that she no longer needed them. But from October to April, coolness and common sense prevailed in her well-ordered mind, and she knew where she was. To be sure, the prospect of another Christmas alone at the Biedermeier kept her slightly on edge, but on the whole, winter was Katherine's season.

It was not that Katherine disliked Christmas in New York. The city took on a splendid blue-and-silver look during that season, people on the street seemed friendlier, children higher-strung than usual from the strain of good behavior, and Mrs. Mossler had introduced her to the marvelous tradition of eating lacquered-looking Chinese duck on the day itself. There were always a few stragglers left behind at the Biedermeier for Christmas, and they usually made a jolly informal party together. It was the uncertainty of not knowing whether she would hear from any of the other Heaps that made her tense. She had not been back to Ohio, nor seen the sight of a single face from home, since quitting it more than ten years ago. Only her mother had seen her off at the station, keeping the rest of Katherine's much younger siblings at home with their father. She had not, in fact, even boarded to see her off, had only retreated to wait in the lounge after briefly and unhappily shaking her hand. Katherine had been no more than a few months sober at the time, and knew only too well that she hardly deserved even the handshake.

In the years since, Katherine had offered her parents an

attempt at what AA called making amends, something that encompassed both formal apology and a repayment plan for all she had cost them. Their response had been gracious, polite, even cheering, but Katherine was nonetheless persuaded that they had been repulsed by it, possibly more repulsed by her mentioning while sober what she had long ago done drunk. Certainly when she then asked if they thought she should make amends with her younger brothers and sisters, they nearly shouted—or came as close as any Heaps did to shouting—that it would not be necessary, that the children were very well, thank you, and this conversation had been quite enough. For a few years she had corresponded regularly with her mother, hoping to repair what they had lost through diligence and distance, but of the two, it seemed that her mother preferred the distance. Every year, polite but inexorable, Mrs. Heap drew slightly back, and Katherine did her best to keep as busy as she could in December, to keep herself from dwelling on what they might be doing at home. She would almost certainly not be invited to visit this year, but they might call—and Katherine could not decide whether it would be worse if she was away when they called and missed it, or remained in her room for a call that would not come. So whenever she was out of the hotel in December, she was filled with anxiety that she would miss hearing from them, and whenever she was at home, particularly in those minutes before sleep, she was filled with dread that they would never call again.

Of course Advent began in November just as often as it didn't, but it had always struck Katherine as a sign of disorganization in the year to come. The Christmas season contained in December was a lovely splendid little thing, marked off in fat black sure lines on the calendar; the Christmas season bleeding into the final weeks of November was a spiritless, slushy mess, drained and diluted beyond the possibility of either enjoyment or edification. Only after December was properly underway did Katherine get up very early on a Wednesday morning, blindly dress in her pitch-black room, stumble down the hallway to knock on Trude Haslund's door, and walk a mile to Kervan Company Wholesale on West Twenty-Eighth Street, all before the sun rose, for her Advent greens.

Trude had been an unexpected arrival at the Biedermeier only that fall, and worked as a clerical secretary for the Norwegian Seamen's Mission out in Brooklyn. Whereas Katherine was buying only enough to brighten her room, Trude had been tasked with the foliation of the whole church, a nineteenth-century Romanesque pile that occupied a full city block out in Carroll Gardens, and so had begged Katherine to accompany her to the Flower District to help with transport and quartering. She had gotten a head start on Katherine, of course, but even after two weeks of decking, the church still wanted for finery, so together they went to bargain for boxwood sprays, dagger ferns, smilax, dried lotus pods, juniper, silver fir, incense cedar, princess pine, ilex berry, white and red poinsettias in birch baskets, cedar garlands, white pine and amaryllis wreaths, cypress fronds, and silver-painted pine cones, which Katherine thought looked terrible but which sent Trude into transports. They parted ways at the Twenty-Eighth Street station, Trude nearly horizontal under her mass of greenery but entirely cheerful at the prospect of carrying it for the entire ride to Brooklyn, Katherine mostly unbowed under her more modest cargo, but not nearly so lighthearted.

She was arranging the boxwood over her window, hoping that Christmas cheer would follow, when Mrs. Mossler briefly knocked and poked her head around the door. "Pony Express," she called, and laid a white envelope down on Katherine's entrance table. "I can't stay, I've got to deliver something very irregular-looking upstairs to Patricia, and the man said that it's supposed to be refrigerated. Come by my office later and we'll try to figure out what on earth's to be done about the old Palm Court," which had been used to stage tea dances up until twenty years ago and had since been used for occasional storage. Presently it was being used for nothing and crumbling badly; Mrs. Mossler suspected Dolly O'Connor and Nicola Andelin (fourth floor) of hiding "surplus" merchandise from Loehmann's in it before fencing it. This was not in fact true; they merely used it to throw parties and occasionally to hide their lovers, although never at the same time.

After she had finished with the boxwood but before she had quite decided where to display the holly, Katherine climbed down from her step stool and examined the letter. The return read "Helen Heap, Sweetgum Way, Westerville, Ohio." It was the first letter she had received from any of her siblings in years. The last time she had seen them, they were still children, but Helen would be almost twenty now. After considering her room for a moment, Katherine decided the letter would be best read in the Shaker rocker, since it was close to the window and received the most morning light. It might not be a pleasant letter, and only pleasant letters ought to be read in bed. This way if she had to absorb any shock she would at least be upright and firmly supported in the process.

Helen's handwriting was graceless and awkward but earnest. Katherine liked it right away.

Dear Katherine,

I'm almost embarrassed to send this letter at all. It's been such a long time since we spoke and I know I'm mostly to blame for that. I haven't wanted to trouble anyone, and it just seemed easier this way. I hope you'll forgive me. And I hope you're doing well. Mother used to show us some of your letters and told us you were having a very nice time. I'd like to hear about what you've been up to sometime. It seems silly to try to acquaint you with everything that's happened since you left in a letter. I won't try.

I'm going to be in New York City in February. That's why I'm writing you now. I wanted to let you know, and I'd like to see you, if you'd like to see me. I'm sorry not to have written you sooner, but I didn't know what to say. I received my associate's this month and plan to attend the Laboratory Institute of Merchandising next year. It sounds like a scientific institute but really it's a fashion school. I hope you are still at the Biedermeier because that was the only address Mother had for you. I hope this letter finds you well. Would you please send any answer care of Claire Rutledge of Buckeye Street? She is a good friend of mine and will see that I get your letter. It's not that Mother would object to your writing me here but this way will be easier. I will be glad to know somebody in New York.

Yours sincerely,
Helen

There was so much to consider, so much that Katherine might have felt in reading such a letter, that she hardly knew where she was, or what she ought to feel first. She uttered a few hasty prayers for composure and then, when this failed to answer, turned to the next best thing—the telephone on her bedside table. After several rings she heard Arthur's familiar bluff, discourteous greeting:

"Yes? Who's this?"

"It's Katherine, Arthur. I've just had a letter from home. May I see you?"

"You may not. I can't rearrange my whole morning just because you're easily overturned."

"Can I at least tell you about it while I have you on the line?"

"If you make it quick, and don't get maudlin."

"All right," Katherine said. "It was a letter from my sister, Helen. She's eleven—no, twelve—years younger than me. I've only seen her once since she was a kid. It's the first time I've heard from her in a very long time."

"Fine."

"She says she's sorry for not writing sooner, but she didn't know what to say to me. I don't know how much she remembers, or what my parents might have told her."

Arthur said nothing, and she continued: "She says she's going to be in New York later this winter. She's been accepted to a fashion school here. She'd like to see me and in the meantime she wants me to send my letter to a friend of hers, instead of home. I don't know if Helen is staying with her, or if she's afraid Mother wouldn't respect the privacy of her correspondence, if it had my name on it. Arthur, do you think I ought to try to make another amends to her? To Mother?"

"Was there something wrong with the first one you made her?"

"I don't know. I don't think so. I said everything we had planned I should say to her, and of course I finished paying them both back years ago. I even asked her if there was anything she thought I'd left out, or something that was still on her mind, still bothering her, and she said there wasn't. But things still aren't all right between us. She avoids me. They all avoid me."

"It doesn't sound like you neglected to do anything you should have. It just sounds like you don't like how she feels about you now, which isn't at all the same thing. Have you done anything you shouldn't have done toward her since then? Borrowed money, been disrespectful, caused her any trouble?"

"I don't think so."

"Then there's nothing for you to make amends for. You just want her to trust you, and she doesn't. She's entitled to doubt you for as long as she cares to. You're not in the business of getting her to like you again, you're in the business of cleaning up what you've done in the past and being useful to other alcoholics in the present."

Perhaps curiously, this remark did not hurt Katherine's feelings; Arthur's rough assessment of her situation was somehow reassuring, even comforting, in its clarity. She did want to make her mother like her again, and she had hoped to find an excuse for pressing the matter in Helen's letter. Arthur was right.

"It's perfectly understandable that you would want your mother to like you," Arthur said. "Nothing wrong with that, and nothing to feel wrong about. But you can't let that dictate your actions. By all means write Helen back, only don't go any further in your letter than she went in hers."

"But ought I to write her at her friend's house? I don't mean that I think she's doing anything wrong, only it seems . . . it seems awfully close to intentional deceit, on my part at least, toward Mother, and I wouldn't want to—"

"'Be careful not to drift into worry, remorse, or morbid reflection,'" Arthur bawled over the line, "'for that would diminish our usefulness to others.' When it comes to morbid reflection, you're another Narcissus, Katherine. Now go to a meeting and try to be useful to someone whose last name isn't Heap, if you think you can manage it. I'll see you at our usual time." He hung up as he always did, without farewell.

Relieved at being reminded of her duty, Katherine sprang out of her rocker, as light as a feather. The holly would have to wait.

DICK BUTTON'S
ICE-TRAVAGANZA

Chapter Three

If Lucianne had been at all worried about overregulating, about setting too strict a standard to attract much interest from the men of her acquaintance, her fears had been eased by the time she placed her third telephone call.

"Hello, Court? Yes, it's Lucianne. Fine, all fine. Listen, I'm sorry to be calling so late, only I didn't have the idea any sooner, so I couldn't have. Would you like to make a little money? It's nothing strenuous."

After three consecutive replies of "Well, I don't know—I'd rather make a lot," she changed the question to "How would you like to make some money?" This was answered just fine. Before midnight she had a small but exclusive stable of willing cavaliers, a month's worth of dinners, dances, receptions, and hunt breakfasts on the books, and an extremely large collection of interested parties of the second part, even more exclusive than the first. Nearly everyone she phoned was as eager as she had been: the men because, as a rule, they didn't like to work, and because attending deb receptions on one's own time could be a bore, while attending those same parties as a professional companion, whose civilities were in such high demand as to command competitive rates, made them feel extremely killing.

A few of her best candidates were immensely popular already, and somewhat reluctant to give up a few nights a week for the entertainment of girls they couldn't possibly succeed with, but Lucianne knew how to handle them, too:

"Dear heart, you'd be an idiot to pass up this kind of money. You could do this standing on your head. In fact, you do it for free all the time to begin with. Look at it this way: We both know if you wanted you could very easily get a nice girl interested in going out with you every night of the week, but you couldn't possibly afford to show them all a good time. And if you want to take out the not-so-nice girls, they're even more expensive, and not half so understanding. . . . So why not let two girls a week pay for the other five? . . . And with Christmas coming up, too, I don't know how I'm going to manage half my Christmas list without this. . . . Well, of course I take a cut, darling, because I'm the one running the whole concern. . . . Sure, it's a good idea. Hal Boylston is doing it. . . . I just got off the phone with him not ten minutes ago. He thinks it's a scream."

If Hal didn't clinch it, then hearing about the secret envelopes almost always settled it for the undecided: "She gives you two of them, discreetly, at the start of the evening—one is for expenses only, and the other one has your fee. For heaven's sake don't look at the second one. Just put it in your jacket pocket and forget about it, or wait until she's powdering her nose if you can't help yourself."

Holtie Staples, who was a devoted reader of spy fiction, thought it might be an even better idea to use dead-letter drops "in the interest of operational security," but Lucianne managed to dissuade him.

"Well, I love it, Holtie, only what if somebody else finds it before you get there? New York is a pretty busy place, and I don't think these girls can afford to pay twice."

But the crown jewel in her collection had been Thomas Beall, a young man she had met earlier that autumn, during the long night of the East Coast blackout. He had been a last-minute addition to a group of her friends from the *New York State Conservationist* at a fatted-calf dinner for someone she knew who was being promoted, or possibly posted abroad, where he had made a decisively congenial impression on her. He had been correctly dressed, with the slightly startling addition of a slim brocade tie. Fortunately, nothing else about his conversation or bearing betrayed a desire to appear conspicuous, so she could forgive and even contemplate appreciating the tie. His company remained excellent even after the lights went out during the cocktail hour. The evening was only slightly handicapped by the darkness; they seated themselves by candlelight, and most of the dishes were kept reasonably warm over some old Sterno cans Dot Livingstone had found tucked away in an old pantry closet.

Thomas was slightly taller than average, with very dark brushed-back hair, and spoke with a pleasant baritone. He was a Tidewater Southerner like herself, though without a trace of an accent. They knew quite a few of the same people, and even liked some of the same ones. He might have been a year or two younger than Lucianne, or perhaps five or six; they both tactfully shied away from the subject. She was not self-conscious about her age, but she was certainly aware that it could no longer benefit her socially, though it had not as yet begun to count against her.

She looked him up in the Register later that night after he saw her home, and while his chain of associations was brief, it nevertheless trailed clouds of glory after it (the Union Club, St. Albans, Duke, American Yacht Club). He had called the next day to ask her to see *Man of La Mancha*, which was playing down in the Village.

Ordinarily, Lucianne would not have been tempted to see anything in a warehouse theater, no matter how much she liked the man asking her, but Thomas had assured her that the playwright had both hired and fired W. H. Auden as lyricist, "so that it's bound to be at least as interesting as it is awful," and Lucianne could never resist a burlesque.

Afterward both agreed the show had been a mess, although one very much worth seeing, that Auden ought to have nothing whatever to do with the theater—"Did you hear his *Elegy for Young Lovers*? The first act is worse than this, if you can believe it"—and argued heartily over his "Shield of Achilles," which Thomas was apt to defend.

"I don't mind pacifists if they've got guts," said Lucianne, "but they should never write poetry. And yet that seems to be about all they *do* want to write."

Thomas had wanted to know which pacifists she thought did have guts. The only one she could think of was Eugene Debs—"and say what you like about him, at least he never wrote poems. And he had stomach."

They had gone out six more times before Lucianne received her Great Idea from Mrs. Mossler. She had been uncertain whether to involve him, but he settled that quickly, calling her less than a week into the agency's formation.

Every room at the Biedermeier came furnished with a Princess touchstone telephone, a compact little bedside model, with a keypad that lit up at night ("It's little . . . it's lovely . . . it lights!" had been the tagline when Bell System first advertised it in 1959), but Lucianne had replaced hers with an old lemon-yellow model 500. She liked her telephone set to feel heavy, so you knew you were having a conversation, and she preferred the dawdling pleasure of a rotary dial to mashing a couple of buttons.

"Lucianne speaking," she said.

"Tom listening," he said on the other end. "What's this I hear about you going into business without me? You've got half the guys I know on your payroll and you haven't said a single word to me. Don't I qualify to round out a few polite dinner parties and squire respectable maidens around hotel ballrooms?"

Lucianne grinned in enormous relief. It was not that she had worried Thomas would disapprove, for he was not the disapproving type, but it seemed a matter of particular importance that he should understand what she was trying to do.

"Just what are your qualifications, sir?" she asked, slightly pinching her nose and switching into her most official-sounding secretarial voice. "Can you dance?"

"Credibly, but not creditably."

"Competent in which?"

"In the ordinary country-club line: foxtrot, waltz, Cuban rumba. I can do a Highland fling if I have to," Tom said. "And I can hitch hike, frug, watusi, and do the chicken walk, if it's called for. Does anybody still do the chicken walk?"

"I don't know, but if anybody asks for it, I'll know to send you their way."

"And if you get me about two or three other fellows, after a few drinks I can usually hold up my end of that funny little dance Zorba did in *Zorba the Greek*."

"That awful man—that wretched little picture!"

"You didn't like it?"

"When they cut that poor girl's throat?"

"I didn't mean that part. But I can do other funny little dances after a few drinks, if that helps."

"Most men can," said Lucianne, reverting to her regular voice. "I don't think it's worth including on your list of especial talents."

"Well, you're the expert. I can jitterbug. Also, an aunt of mine taught me the schottische when I was a boy."

"Are you Scottish? I knew your people are Presbyterians—"

"If all else fails I'll just start hurling the girl around the room while talking to her about the weather. Let me know if I'm going too fast. I'm sure you'll want to write this all down."

"There's not room for more than three or four skills on the page. You're all so accomplished. But I've treasured every word, honest, I have. Your clubs?"

"Not many. The Mamaroneck Frostbite Association, the Metropolitan, and the Holland Society."

"Not the Union?"

"No." He paused. "Who told you that?"

"Nobody," Lucianne said. It was not strictly correct to admit, not even to someone you joked around with, who was an excellent sport, that you had looked them up in the Register.

"And I've got an uncle who was an Odd Fellow in St. Louis," he said. "I don't know why."

"It does seem to be a heavily avuncular organization, doesn't it? I don't know anyone whose father was an Odd Fellow, but it seems to me like half the uncles of my acquaintance belong to the Independent Order, or the Ancient Order, or the Grand United Association."

"They haven't got nearly as much to do with their time, the poor dears," Tom said. "They're not like fathers, who always have offices to go to, ex-wives to battle, children and dogs to circumvent."

"Do you ride?"

"I can get off a horse without falling, but that's about it."

"That's a pity."

"Isn't it? I look very imposing on a horse, too, when I can remember to sit facing the front. But you shouldn't send me out on any dates to the Polo Grounds."

"They tore the Polo Grounds down last year."

"Not really. Did they? I guess it's true that the man is always the last to know about those things."

"And the Jets played there."

"No wonder they tore it down, then. I can sail, if that makes up for my indifferent horsemanship. And I never fall asleep in art galleries."

"And you're aware that this is all work and no play? Dancing seriously and soberly, dining with gravity, and saving any funny business for when you see me afterward?"

"I take my duty seriously," he said. "I will eat free dinners, and dance all night, but all my enjoyment shall be strictly professional."

"Have you a car?"

"No, but I don't mind driving the girl's, if her father's got one. Shall I take you out tonight while you're making up your mind?"

She sent Thomas out that weekend to revive a card party of the Sooysmiths, who returned him with hearty approval. He was an equal hit with Jeanette Gildersleeve at the Marbury-Gildersleeve progressive dinner, with Martha Draper at the Saint Nicholas Society's award ceremony for Whitney North Seymour, and with several others. He was amusing, courteous, and got along with everybody, capable of cranking his personality up or down, as if on a dimmer switch, to perfectly suit whatever the girl wanted from him that evening. Within a matter of weeks he was Lucianne's most frequently requested companion. Only Minnie Francis Drisler declined to repeat their date when she called next, about her cousin Annie Easton's whist party: "Haven't you got somebody else who could take me? Thomas was too easygoing for our family. I need a big man to scare Grandfather with."

Of course Lucianne continued to reserve Tom for her own exclusive, strictly amateur use on Thursday and Saturday nights. He took her to the Pennsylvania Society Dinner and to lunch at the Colony. On one particularly memorable Wednesday he skived off work and took her to the three-quarters-empty World's Fair grounds out in Queens, where they skated in a series of extremely wobbly figure eights for two hours at Dick Button's Ice-Travaganza before stumbling out of the rink and terrorizing Pauline at the Lost Children's Bureau: Tom, throwing the door open wide and shouting, "What have you done with our little girl?" while Lucianne, pressing her hands over her heart, muttered madly, "My baby, my baby, *my baby*," until she collapsed in a heap at Pauline's feet. But they were not thrown out; they could both easily outrun the short-winded middle-aged Pinkerton agent chasing them, and Tom had managed to carry away nearly a dozen crayons in his coat pocket, without crushing a single one.

———··———

Pauline was used to heavy work. All the Lower East Side papers relied on old-fashioned hot-metal typesetting, and she had spent many mornings sweating over the hellbox, skimming the dross as everybody waited for the lead to melt. Filling out coloring books with a bunch of kids—who were usually very cheerful despite being lost, since being lost at a World's Fair, and in someplace as impressive-sounding as the Lost Children's Bureau, is nothing to sneeze at—left her with a lot of time and energy to think things over. And these days she thought about Josephine Marbury. There not many women in the Biedermeier of middle age. Katherine and Lucianne probably came the closest, and neither was thirty-five yet. There were a lot of girls in their twenties, a handful in their thirties, and then practically nobody until you got to the old guard, most of whom were at least seventy. Where all the women of forty and fifty might be living, while interesting, did not concern her at present. What concerned Pauline was how to bridge that mortal gap between thirty and seventy, how to speak to someone in Josephine's position without sounding either falsely cheerful or patronizing. She liked older people, and had always felt comfortable around them, having been raised by her grandparents, but Josephine was not merely a representative of the older generation, but a very particular person, one whose privacy she had already violated. The trespass may have been involuntary, but it was no less real for all that.

She could not now, after having so obviously wounded Josephine's dignity when they had last spoken, try to offer helpful little hints about social services. Josephine would feel all the humiliating weight of her pity, all the more so if she tried to hide it, and interventions of that kind always, always emboldened the person who made that into offering direct advice later, then counsel, then command, then disapproval. It was an inevitable corruption that came from wielding authority that Pauline knew she could not escape, not even with the best of intentions.

But perhaps the problem came from thinking of Josephine as an individual rather than as a class. Hadn't she just been thinking about how many older women, many of them no longer able to work, lived in the building, often separated from the younger residents by a great, polite distance?

Wouldn't many of them also benefit from the same services Josephine was entitled to? And they were entitled to them. It wasn't charity, it was what they were owed. It was the barest minimum of what decency, common decency, demanded— common decency being Pauline's favorite kind.

In less than five minutes, Pauline was in Mrs. Mossler's office, still in her khaki uniform with the sash reading "MATRON," speaking in a worked-up and very nearly angry voice.

"I think it's positively disgraceful that a quarter, at least a quarter, possibly a great deal more than a quarter, of the women living here are past the age of Social Security—who don't work, or can't work, or who spent the past fifty years working and have earned the right to a little peace, women who depend on the hotel for their meals, meals that in the past year have been reduced by half, and yet there's not a single sign, not a single notice, hasn't been a single meeting about all the services the City of New York can offer them, services it's been legally required to offer since at least July?"

At least she thought it had been since July. Pauline had a dim memory of hearing about the Older Americans Act on WINS AM at some time over the summer, but figured there would be plenty of time to confirm the details after making her point.

"Those are home-delivered meals that the state is required to provide, meals which are already being made, which will be thrown into the garbage if this hotel continues to do nothing to inform its residents about their legal rights—to say nothing of the transit passes, legal aid, and I don't even know what else. But they've got rights, you know, Mrs. Mossler, and somebody's got to see to it that they get what they're entitled to."

Mrs. Mossler peered up from her books, astonished but not displeased. Her face looked perfectly innocent and at the same time showed every year of her own age. Pauline became aware she was prating to her elders and blushed.

"I think that's a very good idea, Pauline," Mrs. Mossler said, feeling around for her spectacles. After a moment she located them, decided against putting them on, and began to write on a fresh page. "We should certainly—they should certainly be told. I had no idea. The idea! It's an act, you said? . . . They ought to tell people when they pass laws like that." She changed her mind once again about the spectacles, and carefully wound the wires behind each ear. "Who do you suppose we ought to call about it? I mean, who's in charge of getting the meals delivered?"

"I don't know," Pauline said. She had entirely run out of steam and was more than a little embarrassed with herself. There was really no call to have yelled at Mrs. Mossler, who never needed volume to be persuaded. "But I know a lot of people who work for the city; it shouldn't be too difficult to find out. If I let you know, will you be sure to tell the others?"

"I'd be happy to," Mrs. Mossler said. "But as you seem so impassioned on the subject, wouldn't you like to take charge?"

"I couldn't," said Pauline definitively. Josephine would be sure to detect any sign of Pauline's hand in things—and besides, if she did get too involved, it might become too tempting to think of herself as Josephine's fairy godmother. From there it would be the work of a moment to begin congratulating herself on taking an interest in someone else's suffering, and in no time at all she would become perfectly insufferable, a nuisance, and a busybody.

"But I'm sorry I didn't think of it sooner," she said, "especially when you were so worried about stopping breakfast service. And for shouting in your office."

"Oh, that's all right," said Mrs. Mossler. "It was sort of exciting. I wouldn't want it to happen every day, you understand, but it certainly woke me up. I was feeling a bit coma-ish, lost in the accounts. Comatose."

"Thank you—and thank you for not mentioning I had anything to do with it. It might look . . . I wouldn't want anyone to think I was being nosy, or prying, I mean."

"I see," said Mrs. Mossler, who did not really see at all,

but who could appreciate that Pauline was feeling shy after an emotional outburst and who very kindly wanted to put her at ease. "Well, you just tell me who to call, and I'll do the rest. I *do* wish," she went on, forgetting Pauline was still there, "that it weren't so awkward to ask people about their birthdays. There are a few ladies on the thirteenth floor who might be fifty or who might be seventy-five; it would be so awkward if one were to make the wrong guess. But do you think"—remembering Pauline once again—"that it would be worse to need the meals and not be offered them, because you look too young, or to not need them and be told you look like you do? 'Hello, how's everything, I've noticed you look not only old, but half starved, too. . . .'"

———··———

Katherine had spent so long mentally rehearsing her answer to Helen before putting pen to paper that it was nearly Gaudete Sunday before she had anything to send in reply. She wasn't at all pleased with what she had written, but bearing in mind Arthur's admonition not to include anything more confidential in her letter than Helen had included in hers, and to keep it short and rather to the point, she decided it was better to send whatever she could, as soon as she could, rather than trying to perfect it indefinitely.

As a concession to anxiety, she sent the letter from a collection box on Fiftieth Street rather than entrust it to the Biedermeier's ancient mail chute. Just last month Mrs. Mossler had found a cache of postcards and letters from 1942 wedged between the tenth and eleventh floors: "And so closely written, too, because you remember—don't you remember?—they were rationing paper at the time. I hope none of them were about anything *very* important, because I had to take them to the dead letter office and they don't respect the privacy of correspondence. But on balance I think it would have been worse *not* to forward them, and I very much doubt anyone living here at the time was privy to anything of material interest to national security, although a few of our girls . . . do you remember Molly Haskett? No, she would have been before your time, wouldn't she? . . . A few of the girls typed for the Office of Facts and Figures before they consolidated it with half a dozen others into the Office of War Information. Then of course the combined budget was much too large, so they cut it in half and furloughed everybody."

Dear Helen,

Thank you so much for writing to me. I was very glad to get to read your letter. My thanks also to your friend Miss Rutledge, who I hope will be able to get this letter to you without too much difficulty. I am still living at the Biedermeier, and I work here now, too, as a residential manager. I make sure the inner workings of the building are maintained in good order, look after the meals and the hotel laundry, interview prospective residents, and that sort of thing. It's a fine job and one that's well suited for me, although of course I haven't had very much experience elsewhere.

I want to congratulate you on your graduation. Education is a fine thing, and fashion school must be a very exciting prospect. I hope you'll tell me more about it when you get to the city. Of course I'd like to see you. Have you made any plans for your accommodation here? I would be happy to meet you when you get in, if you'll tell me what train you're taking, but of course you may have that already arranged. I'll write my number here below the signature line. You can call me anytime to arrange a meeting, but only if it's convenient for you.

Please don't blame yourself for anything. You couldn't possibly be any trouble, certainly not to me.

Please give my love to the others, if you think it would be welcome. Of course I understand if that isn't practical just at present.

Very sincerely yours,
Katherine

Sending the letter dispelled perhaps half of Katherine's anxiety, and she took the rest of it with her to church the next morning. The liturgical color of Gaudete Sunday was rose, which marked the turning of the season from penitence to joyful expectation. Advent always began in deep, dark, marvelous solemnity before a slow and blinking progression toward gaiety. The name of the day itself came from the beginning of the traditional reading from Philippians: *Gaudete in Domino semper: iterum dico, gaudete.* Rejoice in the Lord always; again I say, rejoice. It had a snappishly fond air to it that suited Katherine's jangling nerves—*Didn't I tell you to rejoice already?*—and she felt by the end, if not entirely filled with the joy of the Lord which admitteth not sorrow, at least a little better acquainted with it.

The day's epistolary reading had been from Romans, chapter 13:

> Owe no man any thing, but to love one another: for he that loveth another hath fulfilled the law. For this, Thou shalt not commit adultery, Thou shalt not kill, Thou shalt not steal, Thou shalt not bear false witness, Thou shalt not covet; and if there be any other commandment, it is briefly comprehended in this saying, namely, Thou shalt love thy neighbor as thyself. Loveth worketh no ill to his neighbor: therefore love is the fulfilling of the law. And that, knowing the time, that now it is high time to awake out of sleep:

for now is our salvation nearer than when we believed. The night is far spent, the day is at hand: let us therefore cast off the works of darkness, and let us put on the armor of light.

Out of the darkness, into the light; Katherine mentally repeated those words to herself throughout the rest of the day, and even as she turned off her bedside lamp before sleep, she thought to herself, *Out of the darkness, out of the darkness,* more plaintively than she had recited the same words that morning, but with all the same desperate yearning for her heart to be filled with gladness. *Out of the darkness, out of the darkness, let me wake in the joy which admitteth no sorrow.* . . . Then she slept.

———··———

Now it was the third week of December, and Lucianne had called up one of her friends, Frank Newcomb, who worked at the *New York State Conservationist*. Frank had been a member of the dinner party on the night she met Tom. He had declared himself too old and too unsociable for her Guide Escort Service when asked, but he was dependable and smart, and she almost always listened to his advice, although she took it no more often than she took anyone else's.

"Frank, I want to get up a little dinner for Tom's birthday next week," she said, after they had passed a few minutes in friendly, inconsequential chat. "Only I don't know many of his friends, so I thought I'd ask you for a few names, since you both went to Duke."

"That's a nice idea, honey," Frank said. But he said nothing else.

"I think it's a nice idea, too," Lucianne said, laughing a little. "That's why I came up with it. Care to help me out a little?"

"Well, I don't know," Frank said uneasily.

"Well, there were a lot of Duke men there that night, weren't there?" Lucianne said. "Will Nichols, Rick Prentiss, Hack . . . I know it'll be close to Christmas, but don't you think a few people will still be in town?"

"They might be. It's hard to say."

"Would you like to tell me whatever it is you're not telling me?"

"It's not that, Lucianne. . . . I know how much you like him."

"I don't like him so much that I want people to lie to me," she said.

"I'm not sure he was very popular at Duke," Frank said. "I'm not sure any of those guys would care to go to a dinner that was just for him."

"Thanks very much," she said.

"Aw, honey, don't get mad at me. I don't know if they're right or they're wrong, and I'm not saying that there's anything wrong with him."

"Is there anything wrong with him?" Lucianne said.

"I don't know," Frank said, still cagey. "But I think it's a good question."

———··———

Lucianne was still a very good reporter, although without a desk, professionally speaking. She still knew who to call, and when, and what to ask them, and what to suggest in turn that made them think somebody else had already told her the bulk of the story, and that it only remained to them to fill in the blanks around the edges, which made them feel more relaxed and ready to talk. There really was a Tom Beall. And the man she had met really had gone to Duke, and really did work somewhere in the city, although no one was quite sure what he did for a living. He made money somehow; he certainly had it. He lived on Sixty-Eighth Street. But he was not Tom Beall, of that much her callers were certain; Tom Beall had spent the past three months in North Carolina looking after his dying father.

The first thing to do, Lucianne decided, was to find a replacement for Tom as quickly as possible, so that she could still offer the exact same breadth and variety in escorts to-morrow that she had today. Whatever else happened, she would not lose anything professionally by it.

She dangled the possibility after Stephen, who had been clamoring to be put on the list ever since she had let him in on the scheme and he had seen how much money she was bringing in.

"I was born for this," he said. "My mother always said I was too dignified to be a gigolo. Or would have said it, if she'd lived."

"The thing is, Stephen," she said, "I'm not sure you would quite do." For some reason she could not name, she suddenly felt reluctant to make him happy. He already looked too happy by half; happy and handsome and un-touched by seriousness. Stephen was ordinarily quite good at reading her, but he thought this was only her usual play-ful contrariness, which always melted at a suitable moment, after just the right amount of frisking about.

"Oh, but I would," he said. "I would do, honey. I'd do extremely."

"It's not that I doubt your ability to make a charming evening for a girl," Lucianne said, casting a frankly censo-rious eye on him, "or even several charming evenings for quite a number of girls. But I'm not sure you could resist trying to get more money out of them on the side, and I'm not at all sure you could manage to behave correctly from nine until three."

"Until *three*? I thought these were your dignified, drowsy society affairs. Pearls and port and everyone back in their own beds by midnight."

"Oh, it's weak tea nowadays, certainly. In my mother's day a society dance didn't properly begin until eleven and ended in breakfast. But too many men who ought to be properly idle have to show their faces in the office in the morning, so unless we're really going high-hat, everyone takes themselves home a few hours before dawn. And there's nothing exactly wrong with getting into somebody else's bed, provided you like one another and are reasonably discreet about it—but that's only if you're a guest, not an escort. An escort goes home—to his *own* home—alone."

"I could manage that," Stephen said, undaunted. "I could manage that standing on my head. Dance until three, touch my hat to the hostess, share my cigarettes, discreetly mention that I have a grandfather, hurl her decently out of the car and see she lands on her own doorstep, then home to bed like a good boy. And don't work for tips."

"And you dance with her as much as she needs you to," Lucianne said. "If someone else cuts in, that's perfectly all right, and it's perfectly all right for you to spend that time dancing with somebody else if you like, although ideally not the same girl too many times in a row—"

"People don't still cut in at dances, surely?" Stephen said, pleasantly horrified at the idea of such formality, being used to the sort of affairs where it was perfectly polite for a person to grab hold of anyone within reaching distance whose face they liked, or else melt into the nearest group of partnerless bodies.

"We do," Lucianne said. "If there's a tradition to be kept up, we more than likely keep it. We write bread-and-butter letters, we cut in at dances—only on girls to whom you have already been introduced, incidentally, although if you also know the man, too, you might say, 'Your loss, Terry,' if you like. We never crash parties after college graduation, we don't smoke at the table—" Here Stephen protested, and here Lucianne ignored him. "If she takes you to her club, don't, for heaven's sake, try to tip anybody aside from caddies and shoeshine boys, and only precede her to make a way through crowds, get into an elevator, or pick up tickets at the theater. Otherwise you follow her."

"Nothing to it," Stephen said. "I'd be a tremendous asset to you, and I solemnly swear not to ask their mothers if they've got any little odd jobs that need doing around the house for pin money. And I won't even look at their fathers and brothers, nor talk to them, nor share my cigarettes. I'll be virtue on a monument."

"It's patience on a monument," Lucianne said.

"Well, patience is a virtue, too," Stephen said, which was

difficult to argue against. "Give me a chance, at least, Lucy dear."

"All right," she said, leafing through her book of names. "You understand I can't send you to anything that really matters, of course, but I could try you out with a card party or something similarly negligible. Here, I'll give you Lillian Foster Oldershaw. She's got a younger sister out this winter, and her mother's been giving a lot of little parties practically every weekend to draw things out. Lillian's just sick to death of it, but she doesn't want to bring the boy she's seeing around the rest of the family. I think he's Spanish or something."

"Are you sure I'll make much of an improvement?" Stephen asked, smiling. "You know my mother was a Jew."

"For heaven's sake, Stephen," Lucianne said, "if you're not going to take this seriously, just say so and let's have done with it. You've got a Christian surname and a perfectly suitable face, but it won't do you any good if you can't keep up your end of a decent conversation."

"I didn't mean anything by it," Stephen said. "Of course I wouldn't have said anything about it to her."

"If you didn't mean anything by it, then there was no reason to have said it in the first place," said Lucianne, still waspish. "I'm only doing this as a favor, you know."

She was perfectly aware that she sounded as humorless

and self-important as her editor on the day he'd fired her. She wanted to blame Stephen for forcing her into such a position, found that she couldn't, and put down the book. Perhaps it was only at financial extremes that good humor could flourish. The very wealthy and the very poor could both afford to laugh at the world, while everyone else in the plodding, muddling middle . . . but that was ridiculous. Manners were manners, no matter what. "I'm sorry, Stephen. That was ugly of me. Of course you wouldn't have mentioned it to anyone."

"That's all right, darling," he said lightly. "I'd never talk religion with a free dinner on the line." He wore the blank and courteous expression that both of them used whenever the other had wounded them. This happened not infrequently, as both Lucianne and Stephen were well-mannered by habit and unkind by nature.

"It isn't that they're bigots," Lucianne said. "But they'll be thinking about how to be hospitable to you as their guest, and it's your job to think about how to be hospitable toward them, and a joke like that might make them think that you thought that they *were* bigots. And a few of us are Catholics, you know. They're only clannish, like all endangered species, and what they like best are the things they already know. The same people, the same places, the same food. It might sound as if I'm running them down, but I'm not.

Plenty of them are ordinary and dull, just like anybody, but within that sort of framework of repetition, you can create something of real, lasting beauty. Like a beehive or a sonnet." It didn't happen to be beauty that could be easily shared with others, or even explained to them, but it was there nevertheless. They created beautiful evenings, beautiful meaningless, mannerly, and gracious evenings, evenings that ended in drowsy, gallant clouds of dawn goodbyes and a sense that one carried something magnificent and honorable with one back into the ordinary world. . . .

After this spontaneous speech was over, Lucianne seemed embarrassed to have said anything at all on the subject, and returned to her former businesslike attitude. "Here's her card," she said, handing Stephen an envelope, "and your allowance for the evening. But that's just for taxis and headwaiters and that sort of thing. If there's a wine steward you needn't tip him. She's going to want to jump out of the car and swim in a fountain on the way home; don't let her. Since it's your first outing, I'd like you to stop in at my room after you see her home. I'll have your fee for you. If it all goes well, and you'd like to do it again, you'll get paid at the start of the next evening, but I like to make sure of my man first."

"Are you sure you wouldn't rather I come by in the morning? That's rather late for you."

"I always keep society hours at this time of year, even on nights I don't go out," Lucianne said. "It's too much bother otherwise." She sifted through the remaining papers on her desk before lighting on the menu for the Oldershaw dinner, and all professionalism vanished. "*Listen*," she shrieked. "Can you ever believe this menu? Cold filet of sole, of course *they* would. Veal Orloff . . . cold galantine of chicken . . . asparagus vinaigrette, at this time of year . . . pistachio bombe . . . ugh, coffee parfait . . . orange Beatrice—oh, Stephen, you poor thing. I'll have a Bromo-Seltzer standing by if you make it back. . . ."

O GLADSOME LIGHT

Chapter Four

When Katherine heard next from Helen, it was not in a letter but over the phone. Christmas was only days away, and she had been keeping out of her room as much as possible. Ever since the beginning of their correspondence, Katherine had cherished the improbable hope that Helen would be in New York for Christmas, even though she had been quite clear about not arriving until February. She knew this idea was perfectly ridiculous but nonetheless found it impossible to shake. By way of maintaining her composure, she had organized her days without a moment of spare time so she wouldn't be disappointed in her own foolish expectations. She had accompanied Stephen on countless errands, gone on hospital-sweeping missions with other AA members in search of the recently dried-out, and steered them to all her usual meetings. She had exhausted even Mrs. Mossler's liking for company, and visited three separate Christmas night markets with Trude looking for a very particular type of tinned smelt without which, Trude assured her, the celebration of Christmas was simply impossible.

She was just getting back after an informal little exchange of gifts with Posey Becker-Wolfe and Helen Gibran and some of the other girls on the fourth floor, where she had given a canister of Chock full o'Nuts instant coffee, an old paperback of Ruth McKenney stories, and a perpetual calendar, and received a record of *The Dream World of Dion McGregor*, which Posey had presented to her with an enthusiasm so overpowering she seemed almost frozen. Some man living in the Village had recorded his dreams, or been recorded by others while he slept—the sleeve bore the tagline "He talks in his sleep!" over a wobbly drawing of legs in pajamas. Posey knew him, or knew someone who knew him, and had insisted on playing it for everyone. They had listened to his story "The Mustard Battle" together on the floor, huddled together in matching bathrobes and weeping with laughter. Nicola Andelin, who worked at Loehmann's all the

555

year round and defied the Biedermeier trend by absenting herself from work for most of December, had brought eight of them, in every color, saying they were dead stock and the store wouldn't possibly miss them. Dion McGregor had an absurd, emphatic little performer's voice, arch and breathless, and yet there was an unmistakably genuine quality to it—he really *did* sound as if he were talking in his sleep, and not like someone trying to affect it.

The mustard battle starts at—yes—quarter after, quarter after. Is everybody lined up for it? DOES EVERYBODY HAVE THEIR MUSTARD? Do you have your mustard? Do you get it out of the jar? Get it out of the jar! Pick, pick your spot now. Well I think, probably—I don't know, the middle of the forehead. SHALL WE SAY THE MIDDLE OF THE FOREHEAD? IT'S A RINGER. If you're hit in the middle of the forehead, drop, you're dead. Yes. Hair doesn't count, hair doesn't count. Anyplace but the middle of the forehead. Okay. . . . Line up in a big crest. That's it, that's it. Now for God's sake, let 'em have it. Let 'em have it! Foreheads!*

* Remastered from the original tape (Torpor Vigil Records, 2014). Initially released on *The Dream World of Dion McGregor* LP (Decca Records, 1964).

The phone was already ringing when Katherine slipped into her room, still dark and freezing cold, since she'd forgotten to close the windows when she had left for the day (she had a habit of airing out her rooms for fifteen minutes every morning no matter the weather, a habit she had no doubt acquired from some hygienic and serious-minded Germanic forebear).

"Katherine Heap," she said, picking up the phone.

"Hello, Katherine—it's Helen—Helen Heap," her sister said.

"Oh, Helen," was all Katherine could say at first. They were both silent for a moment. "I'm so glad you called. Would you say something else, so I can hear your voice?"

"Oh," said Helen, laughing blithely, "now I can't really think of anything to say. Merry Christmas, of course, I suppose."

"Merry Christmas to you, too, Helen. Have you—"

"I suppose I ought to tell you why I'm calling instead of writing again," Helen said at the same time.

Katherine waited, then said: "Yes, please go ahead."

"It's like this," Helen said, all in a rush. "Everything I told you in my letter was true. I did get my associate's, just like Mother and Dad wanted, and I did get accepted to fashion school, and I am coming to New York in a few months. But I'm not going to the Laboratory Institute of

Merchandising. It's another school entirely. You've heard of the Free University of New York?"

"I'm afraid I haven't," Katherine said. "Is it a fashion school, too?"

"No," Helen said, laughing again. "You've heard of the Krebses? Allen Krebs? Sharon Krebs?"

"I'm sorry," Katherine said. "You've caught me on a subject of total ignorance."

"That's all right," Helen said, "only I expect you probably have heard of them. They're that family who went to Cuba last year, with their little boy, and he got fired from his job at another school. They're starting their own school out of a little storefront on Fourteenth Street. It's completely experimental. It's not like practically anything else. A girl-friend of mine from high school ended up going with a boy who studied at Black Mountain College for a few years before they shut it down, and some of their friends are already headed out to New York to get things started. And in February I'm going to join them."

"It sounds very progressive," Katherine ventured.

"It probably is," Helen said. "I'm not as big on the political side as Susan. That's my friend from high school, Susan Kessel. But it's *exciting*."

"I'm glad that you wanted to tell me this," Katherine said. "I hope it's everything you want it to be."

"I hope so, too. And that's where you come in. You see, Mother is, well, she's pretty strict on us, on all of us, since you left. And Dad goes along with whatever she says. I imagine you knew that."

"I didn't know," Katherine said, "but I think I can guess."

"Well, Mother would never have heard of my coming out to New York in a million years unless it was for something conventional and perfectly safe, only I was never a grade A student or anything, so fashion school was about the best I could do. But I need a place I can send letters from, you know, because I can't let Mother know I'm staying with the Krebses."

"Staying with . . . with the teachers who run the school?"

"They don't run it. It was their idea, but they don't run it. Everybody's staying there. Staying there, teaching there, learning there."

"I see," Katherine said.

"So I was hoping you could sort of give me an address at your ladies' hotel. Like a PO box."

"I could do better than that," Katherine said. "I could give you a room here. I had thought you might want to stay here."

"That's very kind of you," Helen said slowly. "But I wouldn't want to stay at a place like that. It sounds very, well, old-fashioned and sort of lonely. I'm sorry. I couldn't think of a nicer way to put it."

"That's all right," Katherine said. "There is a curfew here, of sorts. It is a little old-fashioned. And the rooms are small."

"So you *do* understand," Helen said. "Then you'll let me forward my letters there?"

"Well, I'd like to," Katherine said. "But I don't think it would be quite right for me to . . . to deceive Mother. You know I haven't always been entirely truthful with her in the past, and how that's . . . how it's hurt her. I couldn't lie to her now, not even part of a lie."

"I see."

"I'm sorry," Katherine said. "I don't mean to suggest that you're doing anything wrong. It's just that it would be wrong for me."

"No, it's perfectly clear," Helen said. "You know she's only so strict on the rest of us because of you, and this is my first chance to go somewhere interesting, to do something I think is exciting—and you haven't been home in ten years, and you'd barely have to do anything to help me, but just the same you've got to put Mother first, even though I've never asked you for anything—"

"Oh, Helen," Katherine said unhappily.

"Never mind," Helen said. "I'm sorry I wasted your time."

"Oh, but it wasn't a waste of time at all," Katherine said. "If you only knew how much I've been longing to hear from you—how many times I've wanted to write, but wasn't sure if I should. There's hardly anything I wouldn't do for you, Helen, only I've sort of used up all the harmless lies a person gets in a lifetime already, so to speak. I am sorry, really I am, and I don't want you to worry that I would tell on you. I just can't do more than that, not with Mother."

"Well," said Helen, a little mollified but clearly still relishing the attitude of righteous indignation, which was new to her, "I suppose it was a lot to ask of you, in your condition."

"Might I see you when you get to town in February?"

"I'm not sure. I'll have so much to do when I get here."

"I don't mind waiting. Or I can help you get settled in. Whichever would be easier for you."

"Well, I guess I might," Helen said, and then in even brighter tones: "And I can just get Susan to let me use *her* sister's address, so everything will be all right after all."

———·———

At first Lucianne had not planned on giving Tom—for she still could not think of him as anything but Tom—a chance to explain himself. But he had cornered her just outside the building, when she could not rely upon the nominal chaperonage of the Biedermeier, and begged her to get a cup of coffee with him. She found she did not want to resist the prospect of an explanation, even as she reserved the right to despise it if she chose, and allowed herself to be steered into a nearby luncheonette.

"You're not a Beall?" she asked stupidly. "Be sure to tell the waiter I want a slice of pie with my coffee."

"No," he said. "All right."

"I'm sorry to hear that," she said.

"Not half as sorry as I am, believe you me."

"What is your real name?"

"You won't like it," he said. "I don't even like it." When she did not answer, he said: "Eugene Polton. My people are from Michigan." The coffee arrived, the pie maybe three minutes later. It was a cream slice, and Lucianne sent it back; she ate only fruit pie with coffee.

"I did study at Duke for two years, for whatever that may be worth to you, although I didn't graduate. That's where I met Frank and all those other fellows you know. They don't know much about it, you see. I told them Polton was a whim of my father's—an old name belonging to some branch of the family that produced only daughters, and would have died out otherwise—but that I really went by Beall, that my name on the registrar's list was something more than a joke but less than an error. I didn't know there really was a Tom Beall or I would have picked something else. I just liked the name Tom, and anything was better than Eugene.

I've never met a Beall. I'd gotten the name from an old West Point regiments list in the library. I'd never traveled out of Michigan before I went east for college. I didn't get along very well with my folks. They're dead now, so I figured it couldn't really hurt them, either. I guess I didn't succeed as well as I thought I had, either, if Frank thought there was something fishy about me. I guess there is."

Lucianne then considered the possibility of adopting a feeling of outrage. She could in that moment sense the remarkable nearness of mortification and hurt, ready to be taken in and cherished with the slightest exertion of her will. In fact she need not have exercised herself at all in this point, if she did not like to, being so beautifully justified and perfectly trespassed against; she had only to wait and do nothing, and outrage would naturally descend upon her. But in the next moment Lucianne found that she did not want to feel outraged, and that self-righteous indignation did not appeal to her in the least in this instance.

He went on before any alternative had a chance to present itself: "And to be perfectly honest, Lucianne, I never intended to tell you anything about it. I'm sorry anyone told you in the first place. I had rather hoped to get away with it indefinitely. I would have changed my name by court order before we got married."

"You should have changed it right away," she said, "as

soon as you started being Tom Beall. It was stupid not to have done it right away. What if I had seen the notice during our engagement? I may not be in good standing with a lot of people at present, but I'm still a newspaperwoman."

"I'd thought of that, too," he said, and there was a suppressed note of triumph in his voice. "I would have published the notice in the *Irish Echo*. No one you know reads the *Irish Echo*."

"Yes, that might have worked," she said.

"I can't help but notice," Thomas said, sensing opportunity, "that you said 'during our engagement' just now. Dare I to hope?"

"You shouldn't press your luck just now, especially not with a joke. But there is a Register office in Detroit," Lucianne said in a considered tone. "It's a Social Register state."

"It's good of you to try to salvage things," he said, shaking his head. "My people are from Marquette—in the Upper Peninsula," he added, when it was clear that Marquette meant nothing to her. "Which is a blasted wilderness, and practically Canada."

"But the problem with Thomas Beall," she said, politely ignoring him, and growing excited despite herself, "was that too much of your story was so easily falsifiable. Easterners keep a lot of records about ourselves, and we're fond of checking them. But hardly anyone in New York knows anything about Detroit. And there's quite a decent club there—the Yondotega—where all the members pride themselves on never admitting they're in it. You get much farther, you see, with a story that's got a bit of truth to it, because you *are* from Michigan, and I'm sure you'd have an easier time pretending to be from Detroit than Annapolis. All you have to do is deny you're a Yondotega man, which is perfectly correct, and everyone will think you *are* one."

"Darling!" he said, reaching for her hand across the desk. "Do you mean to tell me that you don't mind?"

"I didn't say that," she said, pulling her hand back from his. "I do mind it, as it happens. Oh, Tommy, what kind of girl do you think *wouldn't* mind that sort of thing?"

Thomas's face took on a queer, wistful expression. "I know," he said. "I know, and it was a rotten thing to have done. Most of all it was a rotten thing to have done to you, of all people."

"The problem with Tom Beall," Lucianne said, "is that he happens to be a very particular person—a person that you aren't. What you ought to have aimed for is a vagueness and plausibility: a common name, not an eye-catching one, a not-especially-important branch of some good-enough family—something more than forgettable, but not a great deal more than that. You don't want a girl to *want* to go home and look you up on the Register after a date. You want her to feel relieved and well-handled—ought I to be using a marine metaphor? I don't suppose you really sail, do you?"

"That part was true," he said. "I really did sail at Duke."

Lucianne's face lost some of the animation that had slowly been creeping back into it. "There's no need to lie to me now," she said. "It's not as if you can get in trouble with me. I'm only thinking of your future. It's more useful to be honest with me at this point, so we can figure out how honest we have to be for your next act."

"I'm not lying," he said. "Really I'm not. I know that sounds dishonest, but what else can I say? I'm telling you the truth."

"You're talking to a Southerner," she said. "Duke is more than a hundred miles from the sea."

"We sailed on Lake Crabtree," he said.

"Oh, *lake* sailing," she said dismissively, though there was relief in her voice, too. "No tides, no currents, hardly any waves to speak of, hardly any freeboard so you're low in the water—that's just messing about in boats. Which is fine, in its own way," she said, before he could protest, "but don't try to pass it off as anything more than what it is."

She looked at her watch and decided it was too much work to try for outrage. She settled for disappointment. "Thanks for the coffee. I've got to go."

"Will I see you again?" he asked. He looked handsome and well-pressed and penitent; he looked like everything she wanted him to look like.

"You can give me a call after Christmas," she said, considering. "I'll know more then."

————··————

Arthur was far tenderer and more sparing when Katherine called him about Helen for the second time. "I'm sorry," he said, after she'd related the wretched whole of their conversation. "I know how much you had put by in seeing her, and in wanting to do right by her."

"Do you think I did right?" Katherine said.

"I wouldn't like to guarantee it," said Arthur. "It's always possible we might have done something wrong, or stepped on somebody's toes without realizing it. Might be there's more for you to learn about the wreckage of the past when it comes to your sister. But I think you did as much right as you could."

"I know she has every right to be angry with me. But it was one thing, knowing she probably was angry with me, and for something I'm sorry to have done—and quite another having her angry with me now, for something I felt I couldn't have helped. And it's *Christmas*." Katherine began to cry.

This brought an end to the tender portion of the conversation. "It isn't Christmas," Arthur said. "It's not Christmas for days yet. And I will get between yourself and self-pity a hundred times if I have to, Katherine, and scratch at you, too, until you stop pursuing it like a lost love. By God, you can be sorry for what happened, but if you start feeling sorry for yourself then you're a goner. And I can't work with goners. There must be a hundred thousand alcoholics in New York whose families won't speak to them. More, even. Who knows how many more. You can cry in your room about what a poor Christmas this will make, which will change nothing and help nobody, or you can go find another lonely alcoholic whose sisters won't talk to *her* and be useful. Not just useful to her, but useful to her in a way that practically nobody else on earth can be, Katherine, because you know just what it's like. Don't hoard your misery, girl. Put it to work for you, and make it earn its keep. Get yourself a dose of Christmas spirit and get a wriggle on. Now don't talk to me again until you've called five other drunks. And I mean called and gotten ahold of them, and taken them out for coffee, or to a meeting, and make sure you listen more than you talk yourself. I don't mean that mealymouthed, half-hearted business where you call when you're pretty sure nobody's going to be in, and then when nobody picks up you can abandon the whole idea and say, 'Well, at least I tried.'"

Katherine began crying in renewed earnest at the thought of a hundred thousand suffering sisterless alcoholics in the same city. But as these tears were generous, concerned with the distress of others and not only herself, she felt lighter almost right away, and was even able to manage something comprehensible in return.

"And if you haven't got anything to do with yourself on Christmas, come over anytime after two. We're having oyster stew and *flæskesteg* and potatoes Anna. If you want anything else, you'll have to bring it yourself. You might as well bring apple cake or gingerbread, or something."

———··———

It had taken surprisingly little time for Mrs. Mossler to get connected with someone from New York's Office for the Aging. The name distressed her, but only for a moment; they were so rich in programming, so flush with federal infusions of cash, so willing and ready to deliver meals that were really not at all bad—not at *all* bad—better, much better, than what the Biedermeier cooks had been able to produce in the past few years. It was not imaginative, but it was fresh and it was wholesome: biscuits and honey, pork chops and stewed red apples, chicken-and-onion stew, fruit cups and navy bean soup, baked potatoes and coleslaw, and on Christmas Eve there was chopped steak and mushrooms, really very creditably turned out. Someone was always stopping by the Biedermeier with a trolley, and Josephine Marbury was now merely one among those who received.

Only very rarely now—only on an especially clement and sunny afternoon, when she was in particularly high spirits—was she tempted by the sight of an open purse, or an unguarded pocket, only to remind herself that she could . . . no, not even then! Josephine Marbury retired a nearly undetected apotheosis of crime, and once again ate her breakfast in the pleasurable silence of her room.

She shared her Christmas dinner with J.D. Boatwright and Mrs. Mossler, and a very pleasant meal they made of it. J.D. contributed a Nesselrode pie from Café de la Paix, while Mrs. Mossler produced a bottle of Cherry Heering, and against their protests mixed a surprisingly drinkable and exceedingly weak cocktail with sweet vermouth and a few Christmas oranges. J.D., who never drank and never missed the Scotch that was meant to be the main ingredient, pronounced it "Ab-so-lutely killing," and permitted her glass to be refilled twice.

Katherine brought an apple cake uptown to Arthur's, where she was glad to crowd into a noisy, close apartment for a change, and scarcely wondered if the phone might be ringing in her clean and quiet room at home. Lucianne dutifully went to Mass the night before and then spent

Christmas Day in bed with a box of peanut butter crackers and a very dull novel, having first taken her phone off the hook. She was interrupted from her fretting only once, a few minutes before sunset, when Trude Haslund stopped by her room with a little marzipan pig.

"It ought to be properly hidden in some *risengrynsgrøt*," she apologized, "only I don't have anything big enough to cook the porridge in, and Katherine has denied me the use of her hot plate. She says it is only good for toast and little things. But it's not Christmas without an almond present. I have one for every girl who is staying over the holidays, so no one will be left out."

"You should also know," she said just before leaving, in a tone so earnest Lucianne could never work out whether she had been joking or not, "that after the sun goes down today is the beginning of the Christmas Peace, the *julefred*, and it is forbidden to hunt all wild animals until the New Year."

"All right," Lucianne said, strangely cheered by Trude's visit, although she had never liked the taste of almonds.

———··———

Lucianne received Tom in her room, now crowded with schedules, fliers, reminders, menus, dance cards, letters, applications, photographs, and various other forms of social detritus. She did not get up to greet him, and he remained in the doorway, uncertain.

"I think you ought to keep going by Tom," she said without otherwise acknowledging his presence. "It's what I'm used to at this point, and I also think that it suits you. But your surname ought to be something plausible and inconspicuous. Cooper or Holmes or Weld or something, from a properly enormous old family that's been flinging descendants all over the country for centuries. Maryland is too small, and its families too settled. Cooper is plausible, and that's all you need to make this work. Would you mind being Tom Cooper?"

"Good morning, darling," he said, crossing the room instantly and kissing her lightly on the forehead. "That all depends. Would you mind being Lucianne Cooper?"

She shook her head a little, pulling back. "I asked you first, please. Kindly answer in order."

He took off his coat and sat down, pulling it across his lap in a homely, boyish gesture. "I would not mind being Tom Cooper. Especially since it's a name you picked out for me—and, I hope, a name you'll at least consider letting me give right back to you."

"Good," she said, brightening. Now she could look at him, and now she could smile. But the tentative, brittle pleasure animating her face was awful to look at.

"Has it been making you very unhappy?" he asked.

"Yes."

"I'm very sorry."

"I know. How long do you think before you can get it changed?"

"Not long. A few weeks. The offices will be closed now, of course."

"All right. Let's say you go in next Monday. I think the *Irish Echo* was a fine idea. They'll publish the notice for however long it needs doing, and then we can get married in March, if that suits you. Three months is plenty long for an engagement, especially when neither of us are very young."

"We're not old," he said, a little stung—mostly, but not exclusively, on her behalf.

"No, but we're not young. And if anyone we know does see it, you can tell them it was to please an old relative of your mother's, one who's left you a pile of money. Where shall we live? I'd like to stay in the city, if it's all the same to you."

"Luce," Tom said, half rising out of his chair, "you can't be half as angry with me as you sound. Do you mean it? You'll marry me? Even though I'm a liar, and underhanded and . . . and everything?"

"I don't mind that you're a little grasping," she said. "I like graspers. Stop that. Sit back down," and he returned to his seat, half reassured and half annoyed at being rebuffed. "And I even like liars, if they're of the right sort of liar, and especially if they know when it's smarter to tell the truth. And besides, it's Christmas." She leaned forward, looking at him seriously. "*But you should have let me in on it sooner.* That's what I didn't like about it, Tommy. You cheated me of all sorts of fun when you didn't let me in on it. You should have known—from the first day we met, you should have known that I'd have understood, that I'd have helped you. And we could have had a lot of fun doing it sooner."

"I know," he said. "I know that now."

Lucianne's animation had lost almost all of that wounded quality that had so worried Tom at first, although there was still a note of defensive pride as she said: "If we're going to get along together, you ought to know that you really shouldn't lie to me. You might get away with it some of the time. I don't pretend to know everything. But you won't get much out of it, and I'll know you've done it, most of the time—and I'll like you a little less each time you do it."

There was still that unbridgeable channel between them, which Tom could not cross even after Lucianne had agreed to everything, a frostiness he could not melt with a look or a word. Did she mean to send him back out of the room after this? Would she really accept his proposal without even letting him take her by the hand?

"Above all," she said, "I won't be humiliated. That's something you've got to understand, Tommy. I do love you, and I think we could make one another very happy. But I won't let you make me look foolish a second time."

"Not foolish," he said, and this time he would not get up from her side, no matter how much she protested, "not *you*, Luce." He took her hand, he smoothed her dark hair, he murmured inane, comforting, meaningless things, and she patiently let him. "I never thought of it that way, you've got to know that. I never thought I was . . . You were never foolish to me."

"But if you could fool *me*," she said, ignoring what he had said, with real pleasure in her voice, "think of what we could get over on the rest of them. Only think of it, Tom!"

———··———

Like many retirees, Josephine found the adjustment a trifle more difficult than she had anticipated. It had been such an easy way of making a little money, such a solace—and such a trifle, too, since she never swept a purse or wallet clean. There had been no justification for this instance, however; even Josephine had to admit as much to herself. It had been a moment of pure self-conceit. But the temptation had been overwhelming. She had gone out for a walk on a cold and sunny afternoon, during one of those comfortably featureless days between Christmas and New Year's, and without realizing it drifted toward one of her most remunerative "patches," a part of the East River Greenway often frequented by the drowsy and well-off, and could not resist testing her skill against the relaxed vigilance of the peaceable, milling crowds.

She was rarely noticed—she was noticed today. This particular part of Kips Bay still employed its fair share of old-fashioned foot patrolmen, and one of them noticed her now. His name was Brennan and he was no stupider or crueler an officer than the Manhattan average. He scarcely noticed her, only in passing and almost entirely after she had completed the act, but he saw her nevertheless, and his attention was all the more sharpened for not being quite certain of what he had just seen. There had been a number of reported thefts in the park over the past few months, more than was usual for the neighborhood and time of year; it was entirely possible that this little old lady had nothing to do with them, and then again perhaps she did. He too felt his own senses sharpened by the crowd's well-fed docility, and let the thrill of a silent chase outweigh the bother of dealing with it here and now; they therefore both left the victim to discover her loss later and in her own time, and both of them turned toward the Biedermeier.

Officer Brennan did not entirely escape Josephine's

notice on the walk home, however. Once she realized he had followed her onto Second Avenue, she knew with a sinking certainty that she must have been seen. She could not console herself with any fictive hopes that they might be walking in the same direction. Nor did she believe she possessed any criminal skills outside the pickpocketing line; there was no hope of trying to "lose her tail" like they did in the movies by expertly maneuvering through back entrances or barroom windows. She placed all her hope in walking slowly back to the Biedermeier, where if she had any luck someone would stop him at the ground floor. What she would do after that, she did not know. The fact that he would certainly know where she lived if she walked into the hotel now weighed less with her than the fact of getting away from him and indoors as quickly as possible. Being inside the Biedermeier meant being free from the world's attention, a condition she had often regretted in the past but would happily revel in today.

She stepped inside the lobby, which was damnably empty. The elevator for once appeared within seconds of pressing the call button, and Stephen, bless him, stood before her. She hurried inside the cab at once and whispered, "Will you stop at a few floors for me, please? There's a man following me, and I wouldn't like him to see exactly where I live."

Stephen wasn't sure just how seriously to take her. It

seemed unlikely that anyone would be after Josephine for any reason, and yet he had not known her to joke about that sort of thing before. But serious or no, he was always happy to be enlisted in a campaign designed to confuse the enemy; he swept his hat off to her and set a course that would call for every other floor between seven and fifteen.

"I'll take you down to the second floor by way of the freight elevator," he said. "It doesn't have a floor indicator display in the lobby, and we can get off the main line at the seventh floor and let him think we're heading for the penthouse. Would you like me to throw the bum out, once I've seen you to your door?"

Josephine shook her head, clutching her handbag close. "Better not," she said. "I believe he's a police officer."

Once Stephen had escorted Josephine to her own room and heard her locking the door behind her, he walked lightly down the hall until he reached the stairwell behind the elevator banks. Taking a key from his pocket, he opened the door into a musty and rarely used set of fire stairs, and walked smartly up eight more flights before reaching the mechanical attic on the Biedermeier's tenth floor. He had rigged up a private sort of office behind the boiler ages ago, mostly so he could sleep off hangovers in peace, and usually kept a bag of apples and a stack of Mary Renault novels next to the water pump. For a number of reasons Stephen had no interest in meeting a policeman today. He stretched out underneath the quiet hum of the Biedermeier's heating system, arranged his head against the bag of apples, and almost instantly fell asleep.

———··———

Brennan waited for the elevator in the lobby for nearly ten minutes before someone wandered out of the front office—a beautiful dark-haired girl with a face like a junior midshipman, wearing a trim khaki uniform and the improbable badge of MATRON in a sash across her waist.

"Hello," she said politely. "I'm afraid the elevator hasn't been seen to in years. It only works with an elevator boy to work the crank, and Stephen must be out running errands or something."

"You're the matron here?" he asked, gesturing to the sign outside. "I saw this is a women's residence."

"That's right," said Pauline, who had been instructed in the virtues of lying to the police on principle from the tenderest age. "May I help you?"

"I'd like to get upstairs, with your permission," Brennan said. "I have reason to believe one of your residents has just stolen something."

"How awful," Pauline said. "You're quite sure?"

"I really can't say more about it just now, ma'am."

"Of course. Of course. I understand. Would it be all right if I asked who you thought you were looking for, just so I could help you find her? I'd hate to think of her being an influence on the other girls."

"You seem awfully young to be minding so many, if you don't mind my saying so."

"I don't mind it," Pauline said. "I don't mind it at all. I take it as a great compliment at my age. And if Mr. Mossler minds it—ha ha!"

Lightly, Officer Brennan brushed any remaining interest from his mind; if she was much older than she looked, and married, too, then the thrill of the first chase outweighed the possibility of a second. "She's a little old woman," he said, "in a dark suit. Not *very* old, but old, with gray in her hair. Maybe five feet tall. Carrying a big sort of handbag with lots of little flowers on it—"

"I think I know who you must mean," Pauline said, "and she lives—oh, shoot, it's gone clean out of my head. I'd love to let you up, of course, but we absolutely can't have any men above the ground floor unescorted, and we'll have to wait for Katherine to come back so someone can answer the telephone. She won't be more than five minutes, I can tell you. You don't mind? Can I get you a cup of coffee?"

He did not mind; he could use a cup of coffee; it had been that long of a day, and thank you very much, ma'am.

"Now you just stay there and enjoy your coffee," she said. "I'll be right back. Oh, it's awful. I do hope there's been a mistake. Not that I think you've made one, of course—but how too, too awful."

Once Officer Brennan was out of sight, Pauline dashed madly down the hallway for Katherine's room. Thank goodness Mrs. Mossler was out, she thought, not because she would ever have handed a resident over to an officer of the law, but because in her muddled innocence she might not have known how best to mislead one.

"There's a police officer downstairs who's mistaken me for Mrs. Mossler," Pauline said without preamble as soon as Katherine opened the door, "and I'd like to make sure he mistakes somebody else for Josephine, or else she's going to be in a lot of trouble. Can I count on you?"

For a moment, a very small moment, Katherine felt frozen. But no one could object to lying to a patrolman, surely. Not even Arthur could set his face against it, certainly not for a cause as good as the defense of a helpless little old lady. And she had felt so low since her last conversation with Helen—the idea of being asked to lie for a good cause raised her spirits splendidly.

"Of course you can," Katherine said. "Do you think you can entertain him for another minute or two? Let me call J.D. and ask her if she'd like to play Sydney Carton."

J.D. did not look especially like Josephine. To the eye of love they might have been impossible to mistake for one another, but to the eye of a patrolman, who has only really gotten a good look at the back of her head in strong sunlight, one small old woman looks very much like another. And Patrolman Brennan was beginning to dislike this chase; since Katherine had joined their party he had noticed both she and Mrs. Mossler had a tendency to simper and giggle, tilting their heads to the side as they did so, like dogs. They also peppered him with questions about crime, declaring themselves scandalized by everything they heard about it, but all the while displaying an interest so avid that it was perfectly bloodthirsty. Nor did a thorough examination of J.D.'s ("Josephine's") room reveal anything that was in the least bit interesting—only a lot of incomplete manuscript proofs and little tins of cat food.

"For William Rufus," she said. "I have the receipt for them somewhere, if you'd like to see it."

"William Rufus is her cat," Pauline explained, as if Officer Brennan had been an especially backward kindergartner.

"That won't be necessary," said Officer Brennan, looking a little older than he had just a few hours earlier. "Thanks very much, ladies." It took another ten minutes to detach Mrs. Mossler and Katherine from his side, who had both begun to work themselves into a frenzy of anxiety about the possibility of criminals hiding somewhere in the building. When at last he was able to shake the dust of the Biedermeier from his shoes, he had to buy himself two egg creams at the drugstore around the corner to restore his equanimity.

A few hours later, Stephen awoke in pitch darkness when a mouse ran over his foot.

———··———

A merry Christmas on ye, and a very good year,
Long life and health to the whole household.
Your life and mirth living together,
Peace and love between women and men.
Goods and wealth, stock and store,
Plenty potatoes and enough herring.
Bread and cheese, butter and beef,
Death, like a mouse, in the stackyard of the barn.
Sleeping safely when you lie,
and the flea's tooth, may it not be well.

—"New Year's First-Foot Blessing,"
A Dictionary of the Manks Language,
Archibald Cregeen

It was the first week of January, and Katherine was chalking her door for Epiphanytide:

19 † C † M † B; *Christus mansionem benedicat* for "May Christ bless this house"; *IIIK* for Caspar, Melchior, and

Balthazar. Although the names were not in fact Biblical, they were nonetheless traditional, and tradition counted for something. It suggested there was still a connection between oneself and the joys of the past, and Katherine had felt lately so profoundly separated from past joys that she thought she'd better observe as many traditions as she could find.

She was interrupted by Lucianne, who was frowning up at her in deep concentration. She had also stepped on Katherine's only other piece of chalk.

"Katherine," Lucianne said abruptly, "don't you think I had better leave some of my things here, even after I move out? I don't know what I'll do with a single cabriolet chair in our apartment. . . . Practically all Tom's things are Nordic style, chrome and ceramic and ergonomic and perfectly awful. I'll be able to get rid of most of it, but whatever we decide upon ought to be unanimous, I think. I can't stand it when there's a *lady's* room, where one tries to cram everything delicate into a single room that doesn't look like anything else in the house. And we've only got a junior four, you know, so I don't think we can spare the room. . . . Don't you think I'd better leave some of my things here? There are so many empty rooms here, you know, and we both know they're never going to be filled, and it would save me a lot of trouble and expense trying to ship them back home for who knows how long."

"I don't see why we couldn't," Katherine said. "I don't see why you couldn't keep your old room, and the key, too. Would you like to come in and sit down?"

"I wouldn't keep the room, you understand," Lucianne said. "I don't need the bed or the key. I won't be back. It's only for storage, until we can move into a bigger place. Mother can't possibly kick about this wedding forever, and wherever she opens her heart, there her wallet is also. . . . Why don't you keep the key, and once I have need of anything I'll write?"

This last part was delivered in settled, decisive tones, as if Lucianne had just neatly solved a problem that had been troubling Katherine for some time. Treating her own anxiety as if it were Katherine's seemed to bolster her mood enormously, because Lucianne was already in higher spirits than Katherine had seen her in days. After only a few moments of struggling, Katherine really found it very easy not to smile.

"I've already covered everything important," Lucianne went on, "but the armchair, the writing table, and the bureau should still be dusted a few times a year. Just a clean, damp cloth—barely damp at all, really only humid, and soft—for the wood, followed by a dry chamois and a thorough airing-out of the room, although the rest of the time you've got to keep the windows shut and the curtains drawn because the sunlight kills. Never any wax or furniture polish, but you must wear cotton gloves because of the oils on your skin, even on clean skin—and I say 'you' because I don't think you ought to trust the day maids with any of this. Let me know if it's too much for you, because I'm sure I can make time to come downtown to look after it myself, but it really shouldn't take you more than a few hours a year and it'll be awfully out of my way."

"I should add," Lucianne said—she sounded almost hesitant, which was remarkably unlike her—"that Patricia and Carol have left a funny sort of wedding present in my room, and one I couldn't possibly take with me, either. It's the hugest stone sort of . . . You can look after it here just as well as the other things, I'm sure—only its eyes sort of follow you, no matter where you are in the room, and I wouldn't want you to be startled when you first see it. *Really*, Katherine," she added in amazement, "you're not writing any of this down."

"I'm sorry," Katherine said. "I wasn't thinking. Just give me a minute, and I'll find a pen." Before going back indoors to find one, she turned back to Lucianne and said, "You know, there will always be a room for you here, if you'd like. It's not as if we're full up these days."

"If by that remark you mean to imply you don't think my marriage will be a success," Lucianne said, "then you should know you are in excellent company, along with my mother, my sister, three of my aunts, and most of my friends. Perhaps you can all start a mutual admiration society."

"I think a successful marriage can include a little out-of-the-way hotel room," Katherine said blandly. "Besides, I think you'll miss coming down here to quarrel with us now and again."

"As long as that wasn't a crack. I can't stand it when people make cracks," Lucianne said, which wasn't at all true.

"I didn't mean to offend you," Katherine went on. "And I've certainly got no business talking about anybody's marriage. I just meant you can keep your things here as long as you like, and if you want to keep something private for yourself here, you'd be welcome to, that's all. For as long as we're still around, that is."

"If this place is still standing in five years, and they haven't torn it down to make room for an expressway, it'll be a miracle," said Lucianne. "And there's *chalk* all over the floor."

A NOTE FROM THE COVER DESIGNER

The Biedermeier + Thibaud Hérem = the perfect match. When this novella about Christmas at the Biedermeier Hotel was announced, it was clear commissioning *Women's Hotel* cover artist Thibaud Hérem was the way to go.

Hérem cropped in on the Biedermeier Hotel's entrance, layered it with Christmas decorations, and covered the scene in snow. Its treatment feels connected to *Women's Hotel*, but it also invites readers to explore a new take on the Biedermeier full of Christmas spirit.

—*Stephen Brayda*

ABOUT THE AUTHOR

DANIEL M. LAVERY is a former Dear Prudence advice columnist at *Slate*, the cofounder of *The Toast*, and *The New York Times* bestselling author of *Texts from Jane Eyre*, *The Merry Spinster*, and *Something That May Shock and Discredit You*. He also writes the popular newsletter *The Chatner*.

Here ends Daniel M. Lavery's
Christmas at the Women's Hotel.

The first edition of this book was printed
and bound at Lakeside Book Company
in Harrisonburg, Virginia, in September 2025.

A NOTE ON THE TYPE

The text of this novel was set in Fournier, a serif type-face released by Monotype Corporation in 1924. It was based on the typeface of the same name created by French typefounder and typographic theoretician Pierre-Simon Fournier around 1742. With its strong contrast between thin and thick strokes and sparse serif bracketing, Fournier was a "transitional" style of typeface, and anticipated the more severe modern fonts that would debut later in the eighteenth century. Its light, clean design presents well on the page, making it a popular choice for printed matter.

HARPERVIA

An imprint dedicated to publishing international voices, offering readers a chance to encounter other lives and other points of view via the language of the imagination.